AFRICAN WRITERS SERIES

177

Some Monday
for Sure

Denia Warner
'982

Some Monday for Sure

NADINE GORDIMER

HEINEMANN
LONDON · NAIROBI · IBADAN

Heinemann Educational Books Ltd
22 Bedford Square, London WC1B 3HH
P.M.B. 5205, Ibadan · P.O. BOX 45314, Nairobi
EDINBURGH MELBOURNE AUCKLAND
HONG KONG SINGAPORE KUALA LUMPUR NEW DELHI
KINGSTON PORT OF SPAIN

ISBN 0 435 90177 X

This selection first published in the African Writers Series 1976
Reprinted 1980

Filmset in 10 pt Baskerville
Set, printed and bound in Great Britain by
Fakenham Press Limited, Fakenham, Norfolk

TO FELLOW SOUTH AFRICAN WRITERS,
NOW BANNED AND IN EXILE, WHOSE
WORK ENDURES AND WILL BE READ
AGAIN AT HOME

AND TO THE MEMORY OF
NAT NAKASA, CAN THEMBA AND
TODD MATSHIKIZA

Contents

Acknowledgements

These stories were originally published in the following collections:

'Is There Nowhere Else Where We Can Meet?' and 'Ah, Woe Is Me' from *The Soft Voice of the Serpent*, Gollancz 1953
'Six Feet of the Country', 'Which New Era Would That Be?' and 'The Smell of Death and Flowers' from *Six Feet of the Country*, Gollancz 1956
'The Bridegroom' and 'Something for the Time Being' from *Friday's Footprint*, Gollancz 1960
'The African Magician', 'Not For Publication', 'A Chip of Glass Ruby' and 'Some Monday for Sure' from *Not For Publication*, Gollancz 1965
'Open House' and 'Africa Emergent' from *Livingstone's Companions*, Cape 1972

We are grateful to Jonathan Cape for permission to reprint 'Open House' and 'Africa Emergent'.
All these stories have been republished in Nadine Gordimer's *Selected Stories* published by Jonathan Cape in 1975.

Introduction

Stories and novels are works of the imagination; they embody – implicitly – psychological, sociological and political truths. These often are not representative of the personal point of view of the writer himself; in fact, he must set himself to be a kind of medium through which the attitudes of the society he lives in come to light. This is true of my short stories. They reflect the attitudes of various kinds of whites towards blacks in South Africa, and sometimes the attitudes of blacks towards whites, and various relationships between black and white, but rarely my own attitudes, for the simple reason that these would too often represent the exception and not the rule. Few of the white people in my stories belong to that group of white South Africans who visualize and accept freedom for South Africa in terms of a black majority government elected by unqualified franchise. I do.

Making this selection of only thirteen stories from the five short story collections I have published in twenty-five years, I find that the changing subject-matter and even the changing vocabulary in these books reflect the changes in relationships between black and white over these decades, against the background of political events. This came about subconsciously in my work. The very early stories, *Ah, Woe Is Me, Six Feet of The Country*, are about master–servant relationships. They reveal the shameful impotence of paternalism. The use of the terms 'boy' and 'girl' for adult men and women who were black and doing menial jobs, for example, occurs in these stories because this was – and is, though less often, now – the way in which whites in Africa expressed their view of Africans as 'children' – irresponsible inferiors. *Is There Nowhere Else Where We Can Meet?*, also an early story (I could not have been more than twenty-two when I wrote it), seems to me, now, to show the reverse side of paternalism: violence as the only possible form of communication. But the title also asks the question which found some of many tentative answers in the two stories I've chosen from my second collection, *Which New Era Would That Be?* and *The Smell of Death and Flowers*. They were written during the heyday of the multiracial dream that possessed some blacks and whites (including myself) during the Fifties, and that found expression both in a variety of personal relationships as well as in non-violent political action in which blacks and whites co-operated. *Which New Era Would That Be?* reveals, however, a change of focus in my writing: the story is seen from the point of view of the black men, not the white liberals who have dropped in for a visit.

The Bridegroom, from my third collection, has a theme I find has fascinated me in many of my stories: the average white man and woman's lack of consciousness of, or fear of, an unacknowledged friendship with blacks, and their emotional dependency upon them. *The African Magician* (from the fourth collection) although set in the context of independent rather than colonized Africa, takes the theme further. My approach in these stories, as in very many others, is that of irony. In fact, I would say that in general, in my stories, my approach as a short story writer is the ironical one, and that it represents the writer's unconscious selection of the approach best suited to his material.

Not For Publication deals with the imposition of an image by white upon black – in this case the irony lies in the fact that it is not an oppressor's image that the well-meaning white priest and white liberal fighter for the black cause press upon the young black genius, but it proves destructive, nevertheless. *Something For The Time Being* again explores, with irony, the inevitable limits of the white liberal attitude and the usefulness to which blacks could hope to put it in their struggle for liberation. *Open House* and *Africa Emergent* seem to me to reflect, pretty accurately, the early Seventies, the period after the banning of black mass movements and the left-wing black-and-white movements in the Sixties, when liberalism both black and white could be seen to have outlived both its usefulness and its betrayal of the ideals it believed it stood for. Irony was again my method.

I have chosen *Some Monday for Sure* as the general title story because although written and set in the Sixties, and despite the ironies of a political refugee's life that the story recounts, the certainty of the title remains valid: some perfectly ordinary day, for sure, black South Africans will free themselves and rule themselves.

Nadine Gordimer

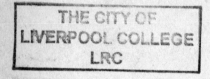

Is There Nowhere Else Where We Can Meet?

I t was a cool grey morning and the air was like smoke. In that reversal of the elements that sometimes takes place, the grey, soft, muffled sky moved like the sea on a silent day.

The coat collar pressed rough against her neck and her cheeks were softly cold as if they had been washed in ice water. She breathed gently with the air; on the left a strip of veld fire curled silently, flameless. Overhead a dove purred. She went on over the flat straw grass, following the trees, now on, now off the path. Away ahead, over the scribble of twigs, the sloping lines of black and platinum grass – all merging, tones but no colour, like an etching – was the horizon, the shore at which cloud lapped.

Damp burnt grass puffed black, faint dust from beneath her feet. She could hear herself swallow.

A long way off she saw a figure with something red on its head, and she drew from it the sense of balance she had felt at the particular placing of the dot of a figure in a picture. She was here: someone was over there . . . Then the red dot was gone, lost in the curve of the trees. She changed her bag and parcel from one arm to the other and felt the morning, palpable, deeply cold and clinging against her eyes.

She came to the end of a direct stretch of path and turned with it round a dark-fringed pine and a shrub, now delicately boned, that she remembered hung with bunches of white flowers like crystals in the summer. There was a native in a red woollen cap standing at the next clump of trees, where the path crossed a ditch and was bordered by white-splashed stones. She had pulled a little sheath of pine needles, three in a twist of thin brown tissue, and as she walked she ran them against her thumb. Down; smooth and stiff. Up; catching in gentle resistance as the minute serrations snagged at the skin. He was standing with his back towards her, looking along the way he had come; she pricked the ball of her thumb with the needle-ends. His one trouser leg was torn off above the knee, and the back of the naked leg and half-turned heel showed the peculiarly dead, powdery black of cold. She was nearer to him now, but she knew he did not hear her coming over the damp dust of the path. She was level with him, passing him; and he turned slowly and looked beyond her, without a flicker of interest, as a cow sees you go.

The eyes were red, as if he had not slept for a long time, and the strong smell of old sweat burned at her nostrils. Once past, she wanted to cough, but a pang of guilt at the red-weary eyes stopped her. And he had only a filthy rag – part of an old shirt? – without sleeves and frayed away into a great gap from underarm to waist. It lifted in the currents of cold as she passed. She had dropped the neat trio of pine needles somewhere, she did not know at what moment, so now, remembering something from childhood, she lifted her hand to her face and sniffed: yes, it was as she remembered, not as chemists pretend it in the bath salts, but a dusty green scent, vegetable rather than flower. It was clean, unhuman. Slightly sticky too; tacky on her fingers. She must wash them as soon as she got there. Unless her hands were quite clean, she could not lose consciousness of them, they obtruded upon her.

She felt a thudding through the ground like the sound of a hare running in fear and she was going to turn around and then he was there in front of her, so startling, so utterly unexpected, panting right into her face. He stood dead still and she stood dead still. Every vestige of control, of sense, of thought, went out of her as a room plunges into dark at the failure of power and she found herself whimpering like an idiot or a child. Animal sounds came out of her throat. She gibbered. For a moment it was Fear itself that had her by the arms, the legs, the throat; not fear of the man, of any single menace he might present, but Fear, absolute, abstract. If the earth had opened up in fire at her feet, if a wild beast had opened its terrible mouth to receive her, she could not have been reduced to less than she was now.

There was a chest heaving through the tear in front of her; a face panting; beneath the red hairy woollen cap the yellowish-red eyes holding her in distrust. One foot, cracked from exposure until it looked like broken wood, moved, only to restore balance in the dizziness that follows running, but any move seemed towards her and she tried to scream and the awfulness of dreams came true and nothing would come out. She wanted to throw the handbag and the parcel at him, and as she fumbled crazily for them she heard him draw a deep, hoarse breath and he grabbed out at her and – ah! It came. His hand clutched her shoulder.

Now she fought with him and she trembled with strength as they struggled. The dust puffed round her shoes and his scuffling toes. The smell of him choked her. – It was an old pyjama jacket, not a shirt – His face was sullen and there was a pink place where the skin had been grazed off. He sniffed desperately, out of breath. Her teeth chattered, wildly she battered him with her head, broke away, but he snatched at the skirt of her coat and jerked her back. Her face swung up and she saw the waves of a grey sky and a crane breasting them, beautiful as the figurehead of a ship. She staggered for balance and the handbag and parcel fell. At once he was upon them, and she wheeled about; but as she was about to fall on her knees to get there first, a sudden relief, like a rush of tears, came to her and instead, she ran. She ran and ran, stumbling wildly off through the stalks of dead grass, turning over her heels against hard winter tussocks, blundering through trees and bushes. The young mimosas closed in, lowering a thicket of twigs right to the ground, but she tore herself through, feeling the dust in her eyes and the scaly twigs hooking at her hair. There was a ditch, knee-high in blackjacks; like pins responding to a magnet they fastened along her legs, but on the other side there was a fence and then the road . . . She clawed at the fence – her hands were capable of nothing – and tried to drag herself between the wires, but her coat got caught on a barb, and she was imprisoned there, bent in half, whilst waves of terror swept over her in heat and trembling. At last the wire tore through its hold on the cloth; wobbling, frantic, she climbed over the fence.

And she was out. She was out on the road. A little way on there were houses, with gardens, postboxes, a child's swing. A small dog sat at a gate. She could hear a faint hum, as of life, of talk somewhere, or perhaps telephone wires.

She was trembling so that she could not stand. She had to keep on walking, quickly, down the road. It was quiet and grey, like the morning. And cool. Now she could feel the cold air round her mouth and between her brows, where the skin stood out in sweat. And in the cold wetness that soaked down beneath her armpits and between her buttocks. Her heart thumped slowly and stiffly. Yes, the wind was cold; she was suddenly cold, damp-cold, all through. She raised her hand, still fluttering uncontrollably, and smoothed her hair; it was wet at the hairline. She guided her hand into her pocket and found a handkerchief to blow her nose.

There was the gate of the first house, before her.

She thought of the woman coming to the door, of the explanations, of the woman's face, and the police. Why did I fight, she thought suddenly. What did I fight for? Why didn't I give him the money and let him go? His red eyes, and the smell and those cracks in his feet, fissures, erosion. She shuddered. The cold of the morning flowed into her.

She turned away from the gate and went down the road slowly, like an invalid, beginning to pick the blackjacks from her stockings.

Ah, Woe Is Me

S arah worked for us before her legs got too bad. She was very
fat, and her skin was light yellow brown, as if, like a balloon
that lightens in colour as it is blown up, the fat swelling
beneath the thin layer of pigment caused it to stretch and
spread more and more sparsely. She wore delicate little gilt-
rimmed spectacles and she was a good cook, though extravagant
with butter.

Those were the things we noticed about her.

But in addition, she had only one husband, married to her by
law in church, and three children, Robert, Janet and Felicia,
whose upbringing was her constant preoccupation. She sighed
often as she bent about her cleaning, as heavy people do, but she
was thinking about the children. Ah! woe is me, she would say,
when the butcher didn't send the liver, or it started to rain in the
middle of the weekly wash, as if, judging from the troubles in her
own life, she couldn't expect everyday matters to go any better. At
first we laughed at the Biblical ostentation of the exclamation,
apparently so out of proportion; but later we understood. Ah,
woe is me, she said; and that was her comment on life.

She worried about her three children because she wanted them
to know their place; she wanted to educate them, she wanted the
boy to have a decent job, she wanted the girls to grow up virgin
and marry in church. That was all. Her own Mission School
education, with its tactful emphasis on the next world rather than
this, had not made her dangerous enough or brave enough or free
enough or even educated enough to think that any place was the
place for her children; but it had emerged her just sufficiently to
make her believe that there *was* a place for them; not a share in the
white man's place, but not no place at all, either: a place of their

own. She wanted them to have it and she wanted them to stay there. She was enough of an uncomplaining realist to know that this was not easy. She was also conservative enough not to ask why it was so difficult. You got to live in this world the way it is, she said.

The things she wanted for her children sound commonplace; but they weren't. Not where she had to look for them.

At first she rented a room for the children in a relative's house in the Location. She paid for their food and went to visit them every Sunday, and the cousin was supposed to see that they went to school regularly and did not wander about the Location after dark during the week; Sarah believed as fervently in education as she feared the corruption of the dark. But soon it became clear that Robert spent most of his schooldays caddying at the golf course – (Why, why, why! moaned Sarah under the disgrace of it – and Robert opened his hand, pink inside like the unexpected little paw of a knowing monkey, and showed the sixpence and tickey* lying there, misted with the warmth of his palm) and Felicia ran screaming about the dark, smoky streets at night, as other children did. It was all right for the others, who were going to be errand boys and nursegirls; but it was not for Sarah's children.

She sent them to boarding school.

Along came the list of things they must have, and the endless low, urgent discussions over the back gate with her husband and the slow passing of folded pink notes and the counting of half-crowns out of a cotton tobacco bag. She spent, not merely a fortune on them – fortunes are things made and lost – but everything she had, her nine pounds in the Post Office, and all of her wages, every month. Even then it was not enough, for the school was in Natal, and she could only afford train fare for them once a year, so that they spent all holidays other than the Christmas one at school, three hundred miles from home. But they were being educated. She showed me their letters; like all children's letters, non-committal, emotionless, usually asking for something. Occasionally I gave her some sweets to send them, and I received a letter of thanks from the younger girl, Janet, in reply; polite, but without the slightest hint of any pleasure that the gift might have brought. Sarah always asked to read the letter, to see, I knew, if it was

* A South African colloquialism for threepence, during the period when South African currency was pounds, shillings and pence.

respectful: that was the important thing. A look of quiet relief would come over her face as she folded it up again. Yes, she would say, there I know they're being looked after.

When Christmas came I felt ashamed to let her rent a room in the Location for the children for the duration of their yearly holiday, and I told her she could have them with her in the yard, if she liked. She put on her black dress and fringed shawl – she clung to a few old Victorian dignities which were not very service-able, but were certainly not as ugly as some of the notions picked up by black women from contemporary European vulgarity – and went to meet them at the station, starting off very early, because her legs were bad again, and she could not hurry. She was away all day, and I was rather angry, but when I saw her coming home with her three children I was conscious of a sense of ceremony in her, and said nothing.

They were remarkably good children. I have never seen such good children, so muted, so unobtrusive in their movements, so subdued in their play. Too good: the girls coming to sit silently in the sun against the wall of Sarah's room, the boy sitting with his bits of stick and stone amongst the weeds along the fence. The girls did their washing and crocheted caps of red wool; their laughter was secret, never come upon in the open, like a stream heard gently gurgling away hidden somewhere in the undergrowth. Their smiles were solemn and beautiful, but ritual, not joyous-ness. The boy didn't smile at all. When I gave him a water pistol some visiting child had forgotten at the house, he took it as if it were a penance. He's put it away in his box, Mam, Sarah smiled proudly. Oh, yes, it's a big thing for him to have that gun, Mam. He feels he's a big man now.

They were not allowed out of the yard, unless accompanied by their mother, or sent on an errand on her behalf. They used to stand at the gate, looking out. Once Robert disappeared for the morning, and came back at lunch time with dust-blurred feet and grass speckling his clothes. Sarah had been complaining all morn-ing: I know where it is he's gone. It's the golf course, I know. It's at the golf course. Her legs were worrying her, or she'd have gone up there after him. In weary martyrdom she gave him a long, hard hiding, but without anger. He cried and cried, as if in a depression, rather than from hurt.

8

It wasn't just violent anger followed by wails.

Sarah talked about the child's escapade for days; it was in the three pairs of eyes, turned up, white, to look at her as she came out of the kitchen door into the yard; it rested upon the neck of the small boy with the sun that lay upon his bent head whilst he played.

Sarah was sadly stern with the children, and she was constantly giving them advice and admonition. The smallest transgression set off the steady, penetrating small rain of her sorrow and disapproval, seeping down all over and about the bright spark of the child. Under the steadiness, the gentle soaking persistence of her logic, the spark damped out. I told her that I thought she was perhaps too hard on the children – that was not quite it, but then I could not be clear in my own mind about what I thought might be happening to them – and she thought a moment, and then appealed, with the simplicity of fact: But they got to come against it sometime, Mam. If they learn now they can't do what they like, it won't make them angry later on. They must learn, she said – hard now – they must *learn*.

I think she bored them very much.

They went back to school, away on the train for another year. Who knows what they felt? It was impossible to tell. Only Janet, the middle one, cried a little. She's the clever one, smiled Sarah, she's going to be a teacher. She's in Standard Five already. Though two years older, and physically a well-developed young woman, Felicia was only in the same class. Plans for her were vague; but for Janet – Sarah could never help smiling in the strength of her surety for Janet – there was a place.

They never came back to our yard. During the year, Sarah's legs got progressively worse, and she had to give up her job. She went to live in the Location, and managed to get a little washing to do at home. But, of course, it was the end of boarding school; on her husband's earnings alone, with the food and rent in the Location to be paid for as well, it just couldn't be done. So the children came home, and lived with their mother, and went to school in the Location. She came to see me, troubled, I could see, by the strong feeling that they had lost a foothold; but seeing a check to their slipping feet and seeking a comfort in the consolation that although their education would not be as good, she herself

9

would be able to train them the way they should go. She sat on the kitchen chair as she told me, slowly settling her legs, swathed like great pillars in crêpe bandage.

She did not come again herself. Her legs were too bad. She sent the children – often Janet alone – to see me. They never asked for anything; they came and stood patiently in the back yard until I noticed them, and then they answered my enquiries very softly, with their large eyes looking anywhere but at me. Yes, their mother's legs were bad. No, just the same like they were before. No, she couldn't take washing any more. Yes, they were still at school. I always had the curious feeling that they were embarrassed, not *by* me, but *for* me; as if their faces knew that I could not help asking these same questions, because the real state of their lives was unknown and unimagined by me, and therefore beyond my questioning. Usually there was an orange each for them, and an old dress or pullover that had imperceptibly slipped below the undefined but arbitrary standard of the household. Each time they came, they were – not a little shabbier, exactly, but a little slacker; a big safety pin in Felicia's jersey, a small unmended tear fraying on Robert's pants. Even Janet, in a raggy short skirt that was a raggy short skirt; not the ironed, mended, stiffly respectable, neat rag that she had always worn before. Well, food and clothes were getting more expensive; I suppose they were getting poorer.

A long time passed without a visit from them. I used to ask the other black girls: How is Sarah? Have you seen Sarah? They didn't like her very much. I don't know, they'd say, offhand. I hear she's sick, her legs are bad.

Sarah's husband isn't working, my girl remarked one day, scrubbing the kitchen table. What, not working? I said. Then how are they managing? *Her* legs are bad, she can't work, said Caroline, shrugging. I know, I said, but they have to eat. The little boy's working, remarked Caroline. He's working in the dairy at the back. She meant he was cleaning up, washing the floor in the handling room.

I asked her to go and see Sarah next time she was in the Location, and find out what I could do to help. She came back and said: Sarah's husband got another job; he was too old for that job he had. Now he's got a smaller job. And is there anything I can do to help Sarah? I asked – Did you tell her? Caroline looked up at

10

me. Her husband's got another job, she said patiently, as if I were incapable of understanding anything told me once.

One Tuesday morning Caroline came in from her ironing on the back porch and said: Sarah's girl's in the yard – and went back to her iron at once.

Janet was standing under the pepper-tree slowly twisting her bare foot on the stones, and from her stance I thought she must have been waiting there quite a long time. Until Caroline noticed her. Now she said Good Morning, Mam, and came reluctantly to the steps, watching her feet. She wasn't a little girl any longer. The childish round belly had flattened to the curve of hips and the very short, stretched jersey lifted with the quivering new breasts. The jersey was dirty, out-at-elbows. In her very small ears, there were brass earrings with a round, pink, shiny bit of glass in them. She stood looking at me, her head on one side. I hear you've had trouble, Janet, I said, thinking I didn't have to talk to a child, now.

Yes, Mam, she said, very low, and the voice was still a child's voice.

Your father lost his job? I said.

Yes, Mam, she said, shaking her head slowly, like Sarah. There's been trouble.

And Robert's working? I asked.

In the dairy, she said. And looked at her feet.

And couldn't Felicia get a job somewhere? I urged, remembering Sarah's dread of her child acting nursemaid.

She's gone, Mam, said the girl, faintly.

She's what? I frowned to hear better. She's gone to Bloemfontein, Mam, she said, so faintly I could scarcely catch it. She's married, Mam.

Well, that's nice! That's very nice, isn't it? I smiled. Your mother must be very pleased.

She said nothing.

So there's only you at home now, Janet? And you're still at school? Still going to be a teacher, eh? – I was sure that she would smile now, lift up the voice that seemed to be dying away, effacing her, escaping me.

I'm at home, Mam, she said, shyly.

At home?

Yes, I'm home with my mother. – The voice was escaping, struggling to get away into silence.

You mean at home all the time, Janet? I said, in a high tone.

I'm at home with my mother. Her legs are very bad now. She can't walk any more.

You mean you don't go to school at all? You just look after your mother?

Yes, Mam, she said, looking hard at her foot with her eyes wide open. Then she lifted her head and looked at me, without interest, without guile, as if she looked into the face of the sun, blinded.

I said, still in that high tone: Wait a minute, Janet. I've got something for you. I think I've – and escaped into the house. I rushed to the wardrobe, pulled out a dress and an old corduroy skirt and rolled them into a bundle. Halfway down the hall I went back to the bedroom and got five shillings from my purse.

Out in the yard she was still standing in the same position. She hardly seemed to know where she was. I gave her the bundle, saying. Here, I think these will fit you, Janet – and then I held out the money as if it were hot, and said, Give this to your Mother.

Thank you, Mam, she said gravely, and it seemed that she had no voice at all. She tied the money away in a piece of cloth and folded the clothes all over again.

I lingered about the yard, not knowing quite what to do. Caroline was looking at me through the porch windows. Caroline, I called suddenly, Caroline, give Janet some tea, will you?

Caroline never breakfasts until eleven o'clock; it was just time. When I went into the kitchen a few minutes later, Janet was sitting at the table, her face in a big mug of tea, three slabs of bread and jam beside her. I said, All right, Janet? And she took her face out of the mug, and smiled, very faintly, very shyly, with her eyes.

I could hear Caroline talking to her, and presently Caroline came and said: She's going now.

She was standing in the yard again, her bundle in her hand. I came out smiling; I felt better for her. Good-bye, Janet, I said. And tell your mother I hope she'll be better. And you must come and tell me how she is, eh?

There was no answer, and all at once I saw that she was making a tremendous effort to control herself, that she wanted most desperately to cry. Her whole body seemed to surge up with the tears that pushed at her eyes. Her eyes got bigger and bigger, more and more glassy; and then she began to cry, her eyes and nose streamed and she cried great sobbing, hiccuping tears.

What's the matter, Janet, I said. What's the matter?

But she only cried, trying to catch the wetness on her tear-smeared forearm, looking round in an agony of embarrassment for somewhere to wipe her tears. She snorted deeply and gulped and could not find anything. There was the bundle, but how could she use that? How could she cry into that? – in front of me.

But what's the matter, my girl, I said. What's wrong? You mustn't cry. What's wrong? Tell me?

She tried to speak but her breath was caught by the long quavering sigh of tears: My mother – she's very sick . . . , she said at last.

And she began to cry again, her face crumpling up, sobbing and gasping. Desperately, she rubbed at her nose with her wet arm.

What could I do for her? What could I do?

Here . . . , I said. Here – take this, and gave her my handkerchief.

Six Feet of the Country

M y wife and I are not real farmers – not even Lerice, really. We bought our place, ten miles out of Johannesburg on one of the main roads, to change something in ourselves, I suppose; you seem to rattle about so much within a marriage like ours. You long to hear nothing but a deep satisfying silence when you sound a marriage. The farm hasn't managed that for us, of course, but it has done other things, unexpected, illogical. Lerice, who I thought would retire there in Chekhovian sadness for a month or two, and then leave the place to the servants while she tried yet again to get a part she wanted and become the actress she would like to be, has sunk into the business of running the farm with all the serious intensity with which she once imbued the shadows in a playwright's mind. I should have given it up long ago if it had not been for her. Her hands, once small and plain and well kept – she was not the sort of actress who wears red paint and diamond rings – are hard as a dog's pads.

I, of course, am there only in the evenings and at week-ends. I am a partner in a luxury-travel agency, which is flourishing – needs to be, as I tell Lerice, in order to carry the farm. Still, though I know we can't afford it, and though the sweetish smell of the fowls Lerice breeds sickens me, so that I avoid going past their runs, the farm is beautiful in a way I had almost forgotten – especially on a Sunday morning when I get up and go out into the paddock and see not the palm trees and fishpond and imitation-stone bird bath of the suburbs but white ducks on the dam, the lucerne field brilliant as window dresser's grass, and the little, stocky, mean-eyed bull, lustful but bored, having his face tenderly licked by one of his ladies. Lerice comes out with her hair uncombed, in her hand a stick dripping with cattle dip. She will stand and look dreamily for a moment, the way she would pretend to look sometimes in those plays. 'They'll mate tomorrow', she will say. 'This is their second day. Look how she loves him, my little Napoleon.' So that when people come out to see us on Sunday afternoon, I am likely to hear myself saying as I pour out the drinks, 'When I drive back home from the city every day, past those rows of suburban houses, I wonder how the devil we ever did stand it . . . Would you care to look around?' And there I am, taking some pretty girl and her young husband stumbling down to our riverbank, the girl catching her stockings on the mealie-stooks and stepping over cow turds humming with jewel-green flies while she says, '. . . the *tensions* of the damned city. And you're near enough to get into town to a show, too! I think it's wonderful. Why, you've got it both ways!'

And for a moment I accept the triumph as if I *had* managed it – the impossibility that I've been trying for all my life – just as if the truth was that you could get it 'both ways', instead of finding yourself with not even one way or the other but a third, one you had not provided for at all.

But even in our saner moments, when I find Lerice's earthy enthusiasms just as irritating as I once found her histrionical ones, and she finds what she calls my 'jealousy' of her capacity for enthusiasm as big a proof of my inadequacy for her as a mate as ever it was, we do believe that we have at least honestly escaped those tensions peculiar to the city about which our visitors speak. When Johannesburg people speak of 'tension', they don't mean hurrying people in crowded streets, the struggle for money, or the general competitive character of city life. They mean the guns under the white men's pillows and the burglar bars on the white men's windows. They mean those strange moments on city pavements when a black man won't stand aside for a white man.

Out in the country, even ten miles out, life is better than that. In the country, there is a lingering remnant of the pretransitional stage; our relationship with the blacks is almost feudal. Wrong, I suppose, obsolete, but more comfortable all around. We have no burglar bars, no gun. Lerice's farm boys have their wives and their piccanins living with them on the land. They brew their sour beer

15

without the fear of police raids. In fact, we've always rather prided ourselves that the poor devils have nothing much to fear, being with us; Lerice even keeps an eye on their children, with all the competence of a woman who has never had a child of her own, and she certainly doctors them all – children and adults – like babies whenever they happen to be sick.

It was because of this that we were not particularly startled one night last winter when the boy Albert came knocking at our window long after we had gone to bed. I wasn't in our bed but sleeping in the little dressing-room-*cum*-linen-room next door, because Lerice had annoyed me and I didn't want to find myself softening towards her simply because of the sweet smell of the talcum powder on her flesh after her bath. She came and woke me up. 'Albert says one of the boys is very sick', she said. 'I think you'd better go down and see. He wouldn't get us up at this hour for nothing.'

'What time is it?'

'What does it matter?' Lerice is maddeningly logical.

I got up awkwardly as she watched me – how is it I always feel a fool when I have deserted her bed? After all, I know from the way she never looks at me when she talks to me at breakfast the next day that she is hurt and humiliated at my not wanting her – and I went out, clumsy with sleep.

'Which of the boys is it?' I asked Albert as we followed the dance of my torch.

'He's too sick. Very sick, *Baas*', he said.

'But who? Franz?' I remembered Franz had had a bad cough for the past week.

Albert did not answer; he had given me the path, and was walking along beside me in the tall dead grass. When the light of the torch caught his face, I saw that he looked acutely embarrassed. 'What's this all about?' I said.

He lowered his head under the glance of the light. 'It's not me, *Baas*. I don't know. Petrus he send me.'

Irritated, I hurried him along to the huts. And there, on Petrus's iron bedstead, with its brick stilts, was a young man, dead. On his forehead there was still a light, cold sweat; his body was warm. The boys stood around as they do in the kitchen when it is discovered that someone has broken a dish – uncooperative,

16

silent. Somebody's wife hung about in the shadows, her hands wrung together under her apron.

I had not seen a dead man since the war. This was very different. I felt like the others – extraneous, useless. 'What was the matter?' I asked.

The woman patted at her chest and shook her head to indicate the painful impossibility of breathing.

He must have died of pneumonia.

I turned to Petrus. 'Who was this boy? What was he doing here?' The light of a candle on the floor showed that Petrus was weeping. He followed me out the door.

When we were outside, in the dark, I waited for him to speak. But he didn't. 'Now, come on, Petrus, you must tell me who this boy was. Was he a friend of yours?'

'He's my brother, *Baas*. He came from Rhodesia to look for work.'

The story startled Lerice and me a little. The young boy had walked down from Rhodesia to look for work in Johannesburg, had caught a chill from sleeping out along the way, and had lain ill in his brother Petrus's hut since his arrival three days before. Our boys had been frightened to ask us for help for him because we had never been intended ever to know of his presence. Rhodesian natives are barred from entering the Union unless they have a permit; the young man was an illegal immigrant. No doubt our boys had managed the whole thing successfully several times before; a number of relatives must have walked the seven or eight hundred miles from poverty to the paradise of zoot suits, police raids, and black slum townships that is their *Egoli*, City of Gold – the Bantu name for Johannesburg. It was merely a matter of getting such a man to lie low on our farm until a job could be found with someone who would be glad to take the risk of prosecution for employing an illegal immigrant in exchange for the services of someone as yet untainted by the city.

Well, this was one who would never get up again.

'You would think they would have felt they could tell *us*', said Lerice next morning. 'Once the man was ill. You would have thought at least—' When she is getting intense over something, she has a way of standing in the middle of a room as people do when

17

they are shortly to leave on a journey, looking searchingly about her at the most familiar objects as if she had never seen them before. I had noticed that in Petrus's presence in the kitchen, earlier, she had had the air of being almost offended with him, almost hurt.

In any case, I really haven't the time or inclination any more to go into everything in our life that I know Lerice, from those alarmed and pressing eyes of hers, would like us to go into. She is the kind of woman who doesn't mind if she looks plain, or odd; I don't suppose she would even care if she knew how strange she looks when her whole face is out of proportion with urgent uncertainty. I said, 'Now I'm the one who'll have to do all the dirty work, I suppose.'

She was still staring at me, trying me out with those eyes – wasting her time, if she only knew.

'I'll have to notify the health authorities', I said calmly. 'They can't just cart him off and bury him. After all, we don't really know what he died of.'

She simply stood there, as if she had given up – simply ceased to see me at all.

I don't know when I've been so irritated. 'It might have been something contagious', I said. 'God knows.' There was no answer.

I am not enamoured of holding conversations with myself. I went out to shout to one of the boys to open the garage and get the car ready for my morning drive to town.

As I had expected, it turned out to be quite a business. I had to notify the police as well as the health authorities, and answer a lot of tedious questions: How was it I was ignorant of the boy's presence? If I did not supervise my native quarters, how did I know that that sort of thing didn't go on all the time? Et cetera, et cetera. And when I flared up and told them that so long as my natives did their work, I didn't think it my right or concern to poke my nose into their private lives, I got from the coarse, dull-witted police sergeant one of those looks that come not from any thinking process going on in the brain but from that faculty common to all who are possessed by the master-race theory – a look of insanely inane certainty. He grinned at me with a mixture of scorn and delight at my stupidity.

Then I had to explain to Petrus why the health authorities had to take away the body for a post-mortem – and, in fact, what a post-mortem was. When I telephoned the health department some days later to find out the result, I was told that the cause of death was, as we had thought, pneumonia, and that the body had been suitably disposed of. I went out to where Petrus was mixing a mash for the fowls and told him that it was all right, there would be no trouble; his brother had died from that pain in his chest. Petrus put down the paraffin tin and said, 'When can we go to fetch him, *Baas*?'

'To fetch him?'

'Will the *Baas* please ask them when we must come?'

I went back inside and called Lerice, all over the house. She came down the stairs from the spare bedrooms, and I said, '*Now* what am I going to do? When I told Petrus, he just asked calmly when they could go and fetch the body. They think they're going to bury him themselves.'

'Well, go back and tell him', said Lerice. 'You must tell him. Why didn't you tell him then?'

When I found Petrus again, he looked up politely. 'Look, Petrus', I said. 'You can't go to fetch your brother. They've done it already – they've *buried* him, you understand?'

'Where?' he said slowly, dully, as if he thought that perhaps he was getting this wrong.

'You see, he was a stranger. They knew he wasn't from here, and they didn't know he had some of his people here so they thought they must bury him.' It was difficult to make a pauper's grave sound like a privilege.

'Please, *Baas*, the *Baas* must ask them.' But he did not mean that he wanted to know the burial place. He simply ignored the incomprehensible machinery I told him had set to work on his dead brother; he wanted the brother back.

'But, Petrus', I said, 'how can I? Your brother is buried already. I can't ask them now.'

'Oh, *Baas*!' he said. He stood with his bran-smeared hands uncurled at his sides, one corner of his mouth twitching.

'Good God, Petrus, they won't listen to me! They can't, anyway. I'm sorry, but I can't do it. You understand?'

He just kept on looking at me, out of his knowledge that white men have everything, can do anything; if they don't, it is because they won't.

And then, at dinner, Lerice started. 'You could at least phone', she said.

'Christ, what d'you think I am? Am I supposed to bring the dead back to life?'

But I could not exaggerate my way out of this ridiculous responsibility that had been thrust on me. 'Phone them up', she went on. 'And at least you'll be able to tell him you've done it and they've explained that it's impossible.'

She disappeared somewhere into the kitchen quarters after coffee. A little later she came back to tell me, 'The old father's coming down from Rhodesia to be at the funeral. He's got a permit and he's already on his way.'

Unfortunately, it was not impossible to get the body back. The authorities said that it was somewhat irregular, but that since the hygiene conditions had been fulfilled, they could not refuse permission for exhumation. I found out that, with the undertaker's charges, it would cost twenty pounds. Ah, I thought, that settles it. On five pounds a month, Petrus won't have twenty pounds – and just as well, since it couldn't do the dead any good. Certainly I should not offer it to him myself. Twenty pounds – or anything else within reason, for that matter – I would have spent without grudging it on doctors or medicines that might have helped the boy when he was alive. Once he was dead, I had no intention of encouraging Petrus to throw away, on a gesture, more than he spent to clothe his whole family in a year.

When I told him, in the kitchen that night, he said, 'Twenty pounds?'

I said, 'Yes, that's right, twenty pounds.'

For a moment, I had the feeling, from the look on his face, that he was calculating. But when he spoke again I thought I must have imagined it. 'We must pay twenty pounds!' he said in the faraway voice in which a person speaks of something so unattainable that it does not bear thinking about.

'All right, Petrus', I said, and went back to the living-room.

The next morning before I went to town, Petrus asked to see me. 'Please, *Baas*', he said, awkwardly handing me a bundle of notes. They're so seldom on the giving rather than the receiving side, poor devils, that they don't really know how to hand money to a white man. There it was, the twenty pounds, in ones and halves, some creased and folded until they were soft as dirty rags, others smooth and fairly new – Franz's money, I suppose, and Albert's, and Dora the cook's, and Jacob the gardener's, and God knows who else's besides, from all the farms and smallholdings round about. I took it in irritation more than in astonishment, really – irritation at the waste, the uselessness of this sacrifice by people so poor. Just like the poor everywhere, I thought, who stint themselves the decencies of life in order to insure themselves the decencies of death. So incomprehensible to people like Lerice and me, who regard life as something to be spent extravagantly and, if we think about death at all, regard it as the final bankruptcy.

The servants don't work on Saturday afternoon anyway, so it was a good day for the funeral. Petrus and his father had borrowed our donkey cart to fetch the coffin from the city, where, Petrus told Lerice on their return, everything was 'nice' – the coffin waiting for them, already sealed up to save them from what must have been a rather unpleasant sight after two weeks' interment. (It had taken all that time for the authorities and the under-taker to make the final arrangements for moving the body.) All morning, the coffin lay in Petrus's hut, awaiting the trip to the little old burial ground, just outside the eastern boundary of our farm, that was a relic of the days when this was a real farming district rather than a fashionable rural estate. It was pure chance that I happened to be down there near the fence when the procession came past; once again Lerice had forgotten her promise to me and had made the house uninhabitable on a Saturday afternoon. I had come home and been infuriated to find her in a pair of filthy old slacks and with her hair uncombed since the night before, having all the varnish scraped off the living-room floor, if you please. So I had taken my No. 8 iron and gone off to practise my approach shots. In my annoyance, I had forgotten about the funeral, and was reminded only when I saw the procession coming up the path along the outside of the fence towards me; from where I was standing, you can see the graves quite clearly, and that day the sun glinted on bits of broken pottery, a lopsided homemade cross, and jam jars brown with rain water and dead flowers.

I felt a little awkward, and did not know whether to go on hitting my golf ball or stop at least until the whole gathering was decently past. The donkey cart creaks and screeches with every revolution of the wheels, and it came along in a slow, halting fashion somehow peculiarly suited to the two donkeys who drew it, their little potbellies rubbed and rough, their heads sunk between the shafts, and their ears flattened back with an air submissive and downcast; peculiarly suited, too, to the group of men and women who came along slowly behind. The patient ass. Watching, I thought, You can see now why the creature became a Biblical symbol. Then the procession drew level with me and stopped, so I had to put down my club. The coffin was taken down off the cart – it was a shiny, yellow-varnished wood, like cheap furniture – and the donkeys twitched their ears against the flies. Petrus, Franz, Albert, and the old father from Rhodesia hoisted it on their shoulders and the procession moved on, on foot. It was really a very awkward moment. I stood there rather foolishly at the fence, quite still, and slowly they filed past, not looking up, the four men bent beneath the shiny wooden box, and the straggling troop of mourners. All of them were servants or neighbours' servants whom I knew as casual, easygoing gossipers about our lands or kitchen. I heard the old man's breathing.

I had just bent to pick up my club again when there was a sort of jar in the flowing solemnity of their processional mood; I felt it at once, like a wave of heat along the air, or one of those sudden currents of cold catching at your legs in a placid stream. The old man's voice was muttering something; the people had stopped, confused, and they bumped into one another, some pressing to go on, others hissing them to be still. I could see that they were embarrassed, but they could not ignore the voice; it was much the way that the mumblings of a prophet, though not clear at first, arrest the mind. The corner of the coffin the old man carried was sagging at an angle; he seemed to be trying to get out from under the weight of it. Now Petrus expostulated with him.

The little boy who had been left to watch the donkeys dropped the reins and ran to see. I don't know why – unless it was for the same reason people crowd around someone who has fainted in a cinema – but I parted the wires of the fence and went through, after him.

Petrus lifted his eyes to me – to anybody – with distress and horror. The old man from Rhodesia had let go of the coffin entirely, and the three others, unable to support it on their own, had laid it on the ground, in the pathway. Already there was a film of dust lightly wavering up its shiny sides. I did not understand what the old man was saying; I hesitated to interfere. But now the whole seething group turned on my silence. The old man himself came over to me, with his hands outspread and shaking, and spoke directly to me, saying something that I could tell from the tone, without understanding the words, was shocking and extraordinary.

'What is it, Petrus? What's wrong?' I appealed.

Petrus threw up his hands, bowed his head in a series of hysterical shakes, then thrust his face up at me suddenly. 'He says, "My son was not so heavy"'.

Silence. I could hear the old man breathing; he kept his mouth a little open, as old people do.

'My son was young and thin', he said at last, in English.

Again silence. Then babble broke out. The old man thundered against everybody; his teeth were yellowed and few, and he had one of those fine, grizzled, sweeping moustaches that one doesn't often see nowadays, which must have been grown in emulation of early Empire builders. It seemed to frame all his utterances with a special validity, perhaps merely because it was the symbol of the traditional wisdom of age – an idea so fearfully rooted that it carries still something awesome beyond reason. He shocked them; they thought he was mad, but they had to listen to him. With his own hands he began to prise the lid off the coffin and three of the men came forward to help him. Then he sat down on the ground; very old, very weak, and unable to speak, he merely lifted a trembling hand towards what was there. He abdicated, he handed it over to them; he was no good any more.

They crowded round to look (and so did I), and now they forgot the nature of this surprise and the occasion of grief to which it belonged, and for a few minutes were carried up in the astonishment of the surprise itself. They gasped and flared noisily with excitement. I even noticed the little boy who had held the donkeys jumping up and down, almost weeping with rage because the backs of the grown-ups crowded him out of his view.

In the coffin was someone no one had ever seen before: a heavily

23

built, rather light-skinned native with a neatly stitched scar on his forehead – perhaps from a blow in a brawl that had also dealt him some other, slower-working injury which had killed him.

I wrangled with the authorities for a week over that body. I had the feeling that they were shocked, in a laconic fashion, by their own mistake, but that in the confusion of their anonymous dead they were helpless to put it right. They said to me, 'We are trying to find out', and 'We are still making inquiries.' It was as if at any moment they might conduct me into their mortuary and say, 'There! Lift up the sheets; look for him – your poultry boy's brother. There are so many black faces – surely one will do?'

And every evening when I got home, Petrus was waiting in the kitchen. 'Well, they're trying. They're still looking. The *Baas* is seeing to it for you, Petrus', I would tell him. 'God, half the time I should be in the office I'm driving around the back end of the town chasing after this affair', I added aside, to Lerice, one night.

She and Petrus both kept their eyes turned on me as I spoke, and, oddly, for those moments they looked exactly alike, though it sounds impossible: my wife, with her high, white forehead and her attenuated Englishwoman's body, and the poultry boy, with his horny bare feet below khaki trousers tied at the knee with string and the peculiar rankness of his nervous sweat coming from his skin.

'What makes you so indignant, so determined about this now?' said Lerice suddenly.

I stared at her. 'It's a matter of principle. Why should they get away with a swindle? It's time these officials had a jolt from some-one who'll bother to take the trouble.'

She said, 'Oh'. And as Petrus slowly opened the kitchen door to leave, sensing that the talk had gone beyond him, she turned away, too.

I continued to pass on assurances to Petrus every evening, but although what I said was the same and the voice in which I said it was the same, every evening it sounded weaker. At last, it became clear that we would never get Petrus's brother back, because nobody really knew where he was. Somewhere in a grave-yard as uniform as a housing scheme, somewhere under a number that didn't belong to him, or in the medical school, perhaps,

24

laboriously reduced to layers of muscle and strings of nerve? Goodness knows. He had no identity in this world anyway.

It was only then, and in a voice of shame, that Petrus asked me to try and get the money back.

'From the way he asks, you'd think he was robbing his dead brother', I said to Lerice later. But as I've said, Lerice had got so intense about this business that she couldn't even appreciate a little ironic smile.

I tried to get the money; Lerice tried. We both telephoned and wrote and argued, but nothing came of it. It appeared that the main expense had been the undertaker, and after all he had done his job. So the whole thing was a complete waste, even more of a waste for the poor devils than I had thought it would be.

The old man from Rhodesia was about Lerice's father's size, so she gave him one of her father's old suits, and he went back home rather better off, for the winter, than he had come.

Which New Era
Would That Be?

❦❦❦❦❦❦❦❦❦❦❦❦❦❦❦❦❦❦❦❦

*J*ake Alexander, a big, fat coloured man, half Scottish, half African Negro, was shaking a large pan of frying bacon on the gas stove in the back room of his Johannesburg printing shop when he became aware that someone was knocking on the door at the front of the shop. The sizzling fat and the voices of the five men in the back room with him almost blocked out sounds from without, and the knocking was of the steady kind that might have been going on for quite a few minutes. He lifted the pan off the flame with one hand and with the other made an impatient silencing gesture, directed at the bacon as well as the voices. Interpreting the movement as one of caution, the men hurriedly picked up the tumblers and cups in which they had been taking their end-of-the-day brandy at their ease, and tossed the last of it down. Little yellow Klaas, whose hair was like ginger-coloured wire wool, stacked the cups and glasses swiftly and hid them behind the dirty curtain that covered a row of shelves.

'Who's that?' yelled Jake, wiping his greasy hands down his pants.

There was a sharp and playful tattoo, followed by an English voice: 'Me – Alister. For heaven's sake, Jake!'

The fat man put the pan back on the flame and tramped through the dark shop, past the idle presses, to the door, and flung it open. 'Mr. Halford!' he said. 'Well, good to see you. Come in, man. In the back there, you can't hear a thing.' A young Englishman with gentle eyes, a stern mouth, and flat, colourless hair, which grew in an untidy, confused spiral from a double crown, stepped back to allow a young woman to enter ahead of him. Before he could introduce her, she held out her hand to Jake,

26

smiling, and shook his firmly. 'Good evening. Jennifer Tetzel', she said.

'Jennifer, this is Jake Alexander', the young man managed to get in, over her shoulder.

The two had entered the building from the street through an archway lettered 'NEW ERA BUILDING'. 'Which new era would that be?' the young woman had wondered aloud, brightly, while they were waiting in the dim hallway for the door to be opened, and Alister Halford had not known whether the reference was to the discovery of deep-level gold mining that had saved Johannesburg from the ephemeral fate of a mining camp in the Nineties, or to the optimism after the settlement of labour troubles in the Twenties, or to the recovery after the world went off the gold standard in the Thirties – really, one had no idea of the age of these buildings in this run-down end of the town. Now, coming in out of the deserted hallway gloom, which smelled of dust and rotting wood – the smell of waiting – they were met by the live, cold tang of ink and the homely, lazy odour of bacon fat – the smell of acceptance. There was not much light in the deserted workshop. The host blundered to the wall and switched on a bright naked bulb, up in the ceiling. The three stood blinking at one another for a moment: a coloured man with the fat of the man of the world upon him, grossly dressed – not out of poverty but obviously because he liked it that way – in a rayon sports shirt that gaped and showed two hairy stomach rolls hiding his navel in a lipless grin, the pants of a good suit, misbuttoned and held up round the waist by a tie instead of a belt, and a pair of expensive sports shoes, worn without socks; a young Englishman in a worn greenish tweed suit with a neo-Edwardian cut to the vest that labelled it a leftover from undergraduate days; a handsome white woman who, as the light fell upon her, was immediately recognizable to Jake Alexander.

He had never met her before, but he knew the type well – had seen it over and over again at meetings of the Congress of Democrats, and other organizations where progressive whites met progressive blacks. These were the white women who, Jake knew, persisted in regarding themselves as your equal. That was even worse, he thought, than the parsons who persisted in regarding *you* as *their* equal. The parsons had had ten years at school and

27

seven years at a university and theological school; you had carried sacks of vegetables from the market to white people's cars from the time you were eight years old until you were apprenticed to a printer, and your first woman, like your mother, had been a servant, whom you had visited in a backyard room, and your first gulp of whisky, like many of your other pleasures, had been stolen while a white man was not looking. Yet the good parson insisted that your picture of life was exactly the same as his own: *you* felt as *he* did. But these women – oh, Christ! – these women felt as *you* did. They were sure of it. They thought they understood the humiliation of the pure-blooded black African walking the streets only by the permission of a pass written out by a white person, and the guilt and swagger of the coloured man light-faced enough to slink, fugitive from his own skin, into the preserves – the cinemas, bars, libraries that were marked 'EUROPEANS ONLY'. Yes, breathless with stout sensitivity, they insisted on walking the whole teeter-totter of the colour line. There was no escaping their understanding. They even insisted on feeling the resentment *you* must feel at their identifying themselves with your feelings . . .

Here was the black hair of a determined woman (last year they wore it pulled tightly back into an oddly perched knot; this year it was cropped and curly as a lap dog's), the round, bony brow unpowdered in order to show off the tan, the red mouth, the unrouged cheeks, the big, lively, handsome eyes, dramatically painted, that would look into yours with such intelligent, eager honesty – eager to mirror what Jake Alexander, a big, fat slob of a coloured man interested in women, money, brandy, and boxing, was feeling. Who the hell wants a woman to look at you honestly, anyway? What has all this to do with a *woman* – with what men and women have for each other in their eyes? She was wearing a wide black skirt, a white cotton blouse baring a good deal of her breasts, and earrings that seemed to have been made by a black-smith out of bits of scrap iron. On her feet she had sandals whose narrow thongs wound between her toes, and the nails of the toes were painted plum colour. By contrast, her hands were neglected-looking – sallow, unmanicured – and on one thin finger there swivelled a huge gold seal ring. She was beautiful, he supposed with disgust.

He stood there, fat, greasy, and grinning at the two visitors so lingeringly that his grin looked insolent. Finally he asked, 'What brings you this end of town, Mr. Halford? Sight-seeing with the lady?'

The young Englishman gave Jake's arm a squeeze, where the short sleeve of the rayon shirt ended. 'Just thought I'd look you up, Jake', he said, jolly.

'Come on in, come on in', said Jake on a rising note, shambling ahead of them into the company of the back room. 'Here, what about a chair for the lady?' He swept a pile of handbills from the seat of a kitchen chair onto the dusty concrete floor, picked up the chair, and planked it down again in the middle of the group of men, who had risen awkwardly, like zoo bears to the hope of a bun, at the visitors' entrance. 'You know Maxie Ndube? And Temba?' Jake said, nodding at two of the men who surrounded him.

Alister Halford murmured with polite warmth his recognition of Maxie, a small, dainty-faced African in neat, businessman's dress, then said inquiringly and hesitantly to Temba, 'Have we? When?'

Temba was a coloured man – a mixture of the bloods of black slaves and white masters, blended long ago, in the days when the Cape of Good Hope was a port of refreshment for the Dutch East India Company. He was tall and pale, with a large Adam's apple, enormous black eyes, and the look of a musician in a jazz band; you could picture a trumpet lifted to the ceiling in those long yellow hands, that curved spine hunched forward to shield a low note. 'In Durban last year, Mr. Halford, you remember?' he said eagerly. 'I'm sure we met – or perhaps I only saw you there.'

'Oh, at the Congress? Of course I remember you!' Halford apologized. 'You were in a delegation from the Cape?'

'Miss—?' Jake Alexander waved a hand between the young woman, Maxie, and Temba.

'Jennifer. Jennifer Tetzel', she said again clearly, thrusting out her hand. There was a confused moment when both men reached for it at once and then hesitated, each giving way to the other. Finally the handshaking was accomplished, and the young woman seated herself confidently on the chair.

Jake continued, offhand, 'Oh, and of course Billy Boy—' Alister signalled briefly to a black man with sad, bloodshot eyes, who stood awkwardly, back a few steps, against some rolls of paper –

'and Klaas and Albert.' Klaas and Albert had in their mixed blood some strain of the Bushman, which gave them a batrachian yellowness and toughness, like one of those toads that (prehistoric as the Bushman is) are mythically believed to have survived into modern times (hardly more fantastically than the Bushman himself has survived) by spending centuries shut up in an air bubble in a rock. Like Billy Boy, Klaas and Albert had backed away, and, as if abasement against the rolls of paper, the wall, or the window were a greeting in itself, the two little coloured men and the big African only stared back at the masculine nods of Alister and the bright smile of the young woman.

'You up from the Cape for anything special now?' Alister said to Temba as he made a place for himself on a corner of a table that was littered with photographic blocks, bits of type, poster proofs, a bottle of souring milk, a bow tie, a pair of red braces, and a number of empty Coca-Cola bottles.

'I've been living in Durban for a year. Just got the chance of a lift to Jo'burg', said the gangling Temba.

Jake had set himself up easily, leaning against the front of the stove and facing Miss Jennifer Tetzel on her chair. He jerked his head towards Temba and said, 'Real banana boy.' Young white men brought up in the strong Anglo-Saxon tradition of the province of Natal are often referred to, and refer to themselves, as 'banana boys', even though fewer and fewer of them have any connection with the dwindling number of vast banana estates that once made their owners rich. Jake's broad face, where the bright-pink cheeks of a Highland complexion – inherited, along with his name, from his Scottish father – showed oddly through his coarse, coffee-coloured skin, creased up in appreciation of his own joke. And Temba threw back his head and laughed, his Adam's apple bobbing, at the idea of himself as a cricket-playing white public-school boy.

'There's nothing like Cape Town, is there?' said the young woman to him, her head charmingly on one side, as if this conviction was something she and he shared.

'Miss Tetzel's up here to look us over. She's from Cape Town', Alister explained.

She turned to Temba with her beauty, her strong provocativeness, full on, as it were. 'So we're neighbours?'

Jake rolled one foot comfortably over the other and a spluttering laugh pursed out the pink inner membrane of his lips.

'Where did you live?' she went on, to Temba.

'Cape Flats', he said. Cape Flats is a desolate coloured slum in the bush outside Cape Town.

'Me, too', said the girl, casually.

Temba said politely, 'You're kidding', and then looked down uncomfortably at his hands, as if they had been guilty of some clumsy movement. He had not meant to sound so familiar; the words were not the right ones.

'I've been there nearly ten months', she said.

'Well, some people've got queer tastes', Jake remarked, laughing, to no one in particular, as if she were not there.

'How's that?' Temba was asking her shyly, respectfully.

She mentioned the name of a social rehabilitation scheme that was in operation in the slum. 'I'm assistant director of the thing at the moment. It's connected with the sort of work I do at the university, you see, so they've given me fifteen months' leave from my usual job.'

Maxie noticed with amusement the way she used the word 'job', as if she were a plumber's mate; he and his educated African friends – journalists and schoolteachers – were careful to talk only of their 'professions'. 'Good works', he said, smiling quietly.

She planted her feet comfortably before her, wriggling on the hard chair, and said to Temba with mannish frankness, 'It's a ghastly place. How in God's name did you survive living there? I don't think I can last out more than another few months, and I've always got my flat in Cape Town to escape to on Sundays, and so on.'

While Temba smiled, turning his protruding eyes aside slowly, Jake looked straight at her and said, 'Then why do you, lady, why *do* you?'

'Oh, I don't know. Because I don't see why anyone else – any one of the people who live there – should have to, I suppose.' She laughed before anyone else could at the feebleness, the philanthropic uselessness of what she was saying. 'Guilt, what-have-you . . .'

Maxie shrugged, as if at the mention of some expensive illness, which he had never been able to afford and whose symptoms he could not imagine.

There was a moment of silence; the two coloured men and the big black man standing back against the wall watched anxiously, as if some sort of signal might be expected, possibly from Jake Alexander, their boss, the man who, like themselves, was not white, yet who owned his own business, and had a car, and money, and strange friends – sometimes even white people, such as these. The three of them were dressed in the ill-matched cast-off clothing that all humble workpeople who are not white wear in Johannesburg, and they had not lost the ability of primitives and children to stare, unembarrassed and unembarrassing.

Jake winked at Alister; it was one of his mannerisms – a bookie's wink, a stage comedian's wink. 'Well, how's it going, boy, how's it going?' he said. His turn of phrase was bar-room bonhomie; with luck, he *could* get into a bar, too. With a hat to cover his hair, and his coat collar well up, and only a bit of greasy pink cheek showing, he had slipped into the bars of the shabbier Johannesburg hotels with Alister many times and got away with it. Alister, on the other hand, had got away with the same sort of thing narrowly several times, too, when he had accompanied Jake to a shebeen in a coloured location, where it was illegal for a white man to be, as well as illegal for anyone at all to have a drink; twice Alister had escaped a raid by jumping out of a window. Alister had been in South Africa only eighteen months, as correspondent for a newspaper in England, and because he was only two or three years away from undergraduate escapades, such incidents seemed to give him a kind of nostalgic pleasure; he found them funny. Jake, for his part, had decided long ago (with the great help of the money he had made) that he would take the whole business of the colour bar as humorous. The combination of these two attitudes, stemming from such immeasurably different circumstances, had the effect of making their friendship less self-conscious than is usual between a white man and a coloured one.

'They tell me it's going to be a good thing on Saturday night?' said Alister, in the tone of questioning someone in the know. He was referring to a boxing match between two coloured heavy-weights, one of whom was a protégé of Jake's.

Jake grinned deprecatingly, like a fond mother. 'Well, Pikkie's a good boy', he said. 'I tell you, it'll be something to see.' He danced about a little on his clumsy toes, in pantomime of the way a boxer nimbles himself, and collapsed against the stove, his belly shaking with laughter at his breathlessness.

'Too much smoking, too many brandies, Jake', said Alister.

'With me, it's too many women, boy.'

'We were just congratulating Jake', said Maxie in his soft, precise voice, the indulgent, tongue-in-cheek tone of the protégé who is superior to his patron, for Maxie was one of Jake's boys, too – of a different kind. Though Jake had decided that for him being on the wrong side of a colour bar was ludicrous, he was as indulgent to those who took it seriously and politically, the way Maxie did, as he was to any up-and-coming youngster who, say, showed talent in the ring or wanted to go to America and become a singer. They could all make themselves free of Jake's pocket, and his printing shop, and his room with a radio in the lower end of the town, where the building had fallen below the standard of white people but was far superior to the kind of thing most coloureds and blacks were accustomed to.

'Congratulations on what?' the young white woman asked. She had a way of looking up around her, questioningly, from face to face, that came of long familiarity with being the centre of attention at parties.

'Yes, you can shake my hand, boy', said Jake to Alister. 'I didn't see it, but these fellows tell me that my divorce went through. It's in the papers today.'

'Is that so? But from what I hear, you won't be a free man long', Alister said teasingly.

Jake giggled, and pressed at one gold-filled tooth with a strong fingernail. 'You heard about the little parcel I'm expecting from Zululand?' he asked.

'Zululand?' said Alister. 'I thought your Lila came from Stellenbosch.'

Maxie and Temba laughed.

'Lila? *What* Lila?' said Jake with exaggerated innocence.

'You're behind the times', said Maxie to Alister.

'You know I like them – well, sort of round', said Jake. 'Don't care for the thin kind, in the long run.'

'But Lila had red hair!' Alister goaded him. He remembered

33

the incongruously dyed, artificially straightened hair on a fine coloured girl whose nostrils dilated in the manner of certain fleshy water plants seeking prey.

Jennifer Tetzel got up and turned the gas off on the stove, behind Jake. 'That bacon'll be like charred string', she said.

Jake did not move – merely looked at her lazily. 'This is not the way to talk with a lady around.' He grinned, unapologetic.

She smiled at him and sat down, shaking her earrings. 'Oh, I'm divorced myself. Are we keeping you people from your supper? Do go ahead and eat. Don't bother about us.'

Jake turned around, gave the shrunken rashers a mild shake, and put the pan aside. 'Hell, no', he said. 'Any time. But –' turning to Alister – 'won't you have something to eat?' He looked about, helpless and unconcerned, as if to indicate an absence of plates and a general careless lack of equipment such as white women would be accustomed to use when they ate. Alister said quickly, no, he had promised to take Jennifer to Moorjee's.

Of course, Jake should have known; a woman like that would *want* to be taken to eat at an Indian place in Vrededorp, even though she was white, and free to eat at the best hotel in town. He felt suddenly, after all, the old gulf opening between himself and Alister: what did *they* see in such women – bristling, sharp, all-seeing, knowing women, who talked like men, who wanted to show all the time that, apart from sex, they were exactly the same as men? He looked at Jennifer and her clothes, and thought of the way a white woman could look: one of those big, soft, European woman with curly yellow hair, with very high-heeled shoes that made them shake softly when they walked, with a strong scent, like hot flowers, coming up, it seemed, from their jutting breasts under the lace and pink and blue and all the other pretty things they wore – women with nothing resistant about them except, buried in white, boneless fingers, those red, pointed nails that scratched faintly at your palms.

'You should have been along with me at lunch today', said Maxie to no one in particular. Or perhaps the soft voice, a vocal tiptoe, was aimed at Alister, who was familiar with Maxie's work as an organizer of African trade unions. The group in the room gave him their attention (Temba with the little encouraging grunt of one who has already heard the story), but Maxie paused a moment, smiling ruefully at what he was about to tell. Then he said, 'You know George Elson?' Alister nodded. The man was a white lawyer who had been arrested twice for his participation in anti-discrimination movements.

'Oh, George? I've worked with George often in Cape Town', put in Jennifer.

'Well', continued Maxie, 'George Elson and I went out to one of the industrial towns on the East Rand. We were interviewing the bosses, you see, not the men, and at the beginning it was all right, though once or twice the girls in the offices thought I was George's driver – "Your boy can wait outside."' He laughed, showing small, perfect teeth; everything about him was finely made – his straight-fingered dark hands, the curved African nostrils of his small nose, his little ears, which grew close to the sides of his delicate head. The others were silent, but the young woman laughed, too.

'We even got tea in one place', Maxie went on. 'One of the girls came in with two cups and a tin mug. But old George took the mug.'

Jennifer Tetzel laughed again, knowingly.

'Then, just about lunchtime, we came to this place I wanted to tell you about. Nice chap, the manager. Never blinked an eye at me, called me Mister. And after we'd talked, he said to George, "Why not come home with me for lunch?" So of course George said, "Thanks, but I'm with my friend here." "Oh, that's O.K.", said the chap. "Bring him along." Well, we go along to this house, and the chap disappears into the kitchen, and then he comes back and we sit in the lounge and have a beer, and then the servant comes along and says lunch is ready. Just as we're walking into the dining-room, the chap takes me by the arm and says, "I've had *your* lunch laid on a table on the stoep. You'll find it's all perfectly clean and nice, just what we're having ourselves".'

'Fantastic', murmured Alister.

Maxie smiled and shrugged, looking around at them all. 'It's true'.

'After he'd asked you, and he'd sat having a drink with you?' Jennifer said closely, biting in her lower lip, as if this were a problem to be solved psychologically.

'Of course', said Maxie.

35

Jake was shaking with laughter, like some obscene Silenus. There was no sound out of him, but saliva gleamed on his lips, and his belly, at the level of Jennifer Tetzel's eyes, was convulsed.

Temba said soberly, in the tone of one whose goodwill makes it difficult for him to believe in the unease of his situation, 'I certainly find it worse here than at the Cape. I can't remember, y'know, about buses. I keep getting put off European buses.'

Maxie pointed to Jake's heaving belly. 'Oh, I'll tell you a better one than that,' he said. 'Something that happened in the office one day. Now, the trouble with me is, apparently, I don't talk like a native.' This time everyone laughed, except Maxie himself, who, with the instinct of a good raconteur, kept a polite, modest, straight face.

'You know that's true', interrupted the young white woman. 'You have none of the usual softening of the vowels of most Africans. And you haven't got an Afrikaans accent, as some Africans have, even if they get rid of the Bantu thing.'

'Anyway, I'd had to phone a certain firm several times,' Maxie went on, 'and I'd got to know the voice of the girl at the other end, and she'd got to know mine. As a matter of fact, she must have liked the sound of me, because she was getting very friendly. We fooled about a bit, exchanged first names, like a couple of kids – hers was Peggy – and she said, eventually, "Aren't you ever going to come to the office yourself?"' Maxie paused a moment, and his tongue flicked at the side of his mouth in a brief, nervous gesture. When he spoke again, his voice was flat, like the voice of a man who is telling a joke and suddenly thinks that perhaps it is not such a good one after all. 'So I told her I'd be in next day, about four. I walked in, sure enough, just as I said I would. She was a pretty girl, blonde, you know, with very tidy hair – I guessed she'd just combed it to be ready for me. She looked up and said "Yes?", holding out her hand for the messenger's book or parcel she thought I'd brought. I took her hand and shook it and said, "Well, here I am, on time – I'm Maxie – Maxie Ndube".'

'What'd she do?' asked Temba eagerly.

The interruption seemed to restore Maxie's confidence in his story. He shrugged gaily. 'She almost dropped my hand, and then she pumped it like a mad thing, and her neck and ears went so red

I thought she'd burn up. Honestly, her ears were absolutely shining. She tried to pretend she'd known all along, but I could see she was terrified someone would come from the inner office and see her shaking hands with a native. So I took pity on her and went away. Didn't even stay for my appointment with her boss. When I went back to keep the postponed appointment the next week, we pretended we'd never met.'

Temba was slapping his knee. 'God, I'd have loved to see her face!' he said.

Jake wiped away a tear from his fat cheek – his eyes were light blue, and produced tears easily when he laughed – and said, 'That'll teach you not to talk swanky, man. Why can't you talk like the rest of us?'

'Oh, I'll watch out on the "Missus" and "Baas" stuff in future', said Maxie.

Jennifer Tetzel cut into their laughter with her cool, practical voice. 'Poor little girl, she probably liked you awfully, Maxie, and was really disappointed. You mustn't be too harsh on her. It's hard to be punished for not being black.'

The moment was one of astonishment rather than irritation. Even Jake, who had been sure that there could be no possible situation between white and black he could not find amusing, only looked quickly from the young woman to Maxie, in a hiatus between anger, which he had given up long ago, and laughter, which suddenly failed him. On his face was admiration more than anything else – sheer, grudging admiration. This one was the best yet. This one was the coolest ever.

'Is it?' said Maxie to Jennifer, pulling in the corners of his mouth and regarding her from under slightly raised eyebrows. Jake watched. Oh, she'd have a hard time with Maxie. Maxie wouldn't give up his suffering-tempered blackness so easily. You hadn't much hope of knowing what Maxie was feeling at any given moment, because Maxie not only never let you know but made you guess wrong. But this one was the best yet.

She looked back at Maxie, opening her eyes very wide, twisting her sandaled foot on the swivel of its ankle, smiling. 'Really, I assure you it is.'

Maxie bowed to her politely, giving way with a falling gesture of his hand.

Alister had slid from his perch on the crowded table, and now, prodding Jake playfully in the paunch, he said. 'We have to get along.'

Jake scratched his ear and said again, 'Sure you won't have something to eat?'

Alister shook his head. 'We had hoped you'd offer us a drink, but—'

Jake wheezed with laughter, but this time was sincerely concerned. 'Well, to tell you the truth, when we heard the knocking, we just swallowed the last of the bottle off, in case it was someone it shouldn't be. I haven't a drop in the place till tomorrow. Sorry, chappie. Must apologize to you, lady, but we black men've got to drink in secret. If we'd've known it was you two . . .'

Maxie and Temba had risen. The two wizened coloured men, Klaas and Albert, and the sombre black Billy Boy shuffled helplessly, hanging about.

Alister said, 'Next time, Jake, next time. We'll give you fair warning and you can lay it on.'

Jennifer shook hands with Temba and Maxie, called 'Good-bye! Good-bye!' to the others, as if they were somehow out of earshot in that small room. From the door, she suddenly said to Maxie, 'I feel I must tell you. About that other story – your first one, about the lunch. I don't believe it. I'm sorry, but I honestly don't. It's too illogical to hold water.'

It was the final self-immolation by honest understanding. There was absolutely no limit to which that understanding would not go. Even if she could not believe Maxie, she must keep her determined good faith with him by confessing her disbelief. She would go to the length of calling him a liar to show by frankness how much she respected him – to insinuate, perhaps, that she was *with him*, even in the need to invent something about a white man that she, because she herself was white, could not believe. It was her last bid for Maxie.

The small, perfectly made man crossed his arms and smiled, watching her out. Maxie had no price.

Jake saw his guests out of the shop, and switched off the light after he had closed the door behind them. As he walked back through the dark, where his presses smelled metallic and cool, he heard, for a few moments, the clear voice of the white woman and the low, non-committal English murmur of Alister, his friend, as they went out through the archway into the street.

He blinked a little as he came back to the light and the faces that confronted him in the back room. Klaas had taken the dirty glasses from behind the curtain and was holding them one by one under the tap in the sink. Billy Boy and Albert had come closer out of the shadows and were leaning their elbows on a roll of paper. Temba was sitting on the table, swinging his foot. Maxie had not moved, and stood just as he had, with his arms folded. No one spoke.

Jake began to whistle softly through the spaces between his front teeth, and he picked up the pan of bacon, looked at the twisted curls of meat, jellied now in cold white fat, and put it down again absently. He stood a moment, heavily, regarding them all, but no one responded. His eye encountered the chair that he had cleared for Jennifer Tetzel to sit on. Suddenly he kicked it, hard, so that it went flying on to its side. Then, rubbing his big hands together and bursting into loud whistling to accompany an impromptu series of dance steps, he said 'Now, boys!' and as they stirred, he planked the pan down on the ring and turned the gas up till it roared beneath it.

The Smell
of Death and Flowers

*T*he party was an unusual one for Johannesburg. A young man called Derek Ross – out of sight behind the 'bar' at the moment – had white friends and black friends, Indian friends and friends of mixed blood, and sometimes he liked to invite them to his flat all at once. Most of them belonged to the minority that, through bohemianism, godliness, politics, or a particularly sharp sense of human dignity, did not care about the difference in one another's skins. But there were always one or two – white ones – who came, like tourists, to see the sight, and to show that they did not care, and one or two black or brown or Indian ones who found themselves paralysed by the very ease with which the white guests accepted them.

One of the several groups that huddled to talk, like people sheltering beneath a cliff, on divans and hard borrowed chairs in the shadow of the dancers, was dominated by a man in a grey suit, Malcolm Barker. 'Why not pay the fine and have done with it. then?' he was saying.

The two people to whom he was talking were silent a moment, so that the haphazard noisiness of the room and the organized wail of the gramophone suddenly burst in irrelevantly upon the conversation. The pretty brunette said, in her quick, officious voice, 'Well, it wouldn't be the same for Jessica Malherbe. It's not quite the same thing, you see . . .' Her stiff, mascaraed lashes flickered an appeal – for confirmation, and for sympathy because of the impossibility of explaining – at a man whose gingerish whiskers and flattened, low-set ears made him look like an angry tomcat.

'It's a matter of principle', he said to Malcolm Barker.

'Oh, quite, I see', Malcolm conceded. 'For someone like this

Malherbe woman, paying the fine's one thing; sitting in prison for three weeks is another.'

The brunette rapidly crossed and then uncrossed her legs. 'It's not even quite that,' she said. 'Not the unpleasantness of being in prison. Not a sort of martyrdom on Jessica's part. Just the *principle*.' At that moment a black hand came out from the crush of dancers bumping round and pulled the woman to her feet; she went off, and as she danced she talked with staccato animation to her African partner, who kept his lids half lowered over his eyes while she followed his gentle shuffle. The ginger-whiskered man got up without a word and went swiftly through the dancers to the 'bar', a kitchen table covered with beer and gin bottles, at the other end of the small room.

'*Satyagraha*', said Malcolm Barker, like the infidel pronouncing with satisfaction the holy word that the believers hesitate to defile.

A very large and plain African woman sitting next to him smiled at him hugely and eagerly out of shyness, not having the slightest idea what he had said.

He smiled back at her for a moment, as if to hypnotize the onrush of some frightening animal. Then, suddenly, he leaned over and asked in a special, loud, slow voice, 'What do you do? Are you a teacher?'

Before the woman could answer, Malcolm Barker's young sister-in-law, a girl who had been sitting silent, pink and cold as a porcelain figure, on the window sill behind his back, leaned her hand for balance on his chair and said urgently, near his ear, 'Has Jessica Malherbe really been in prison?'

'Yes, in Port Elizabeth. And in Durban, they tell me. And now she's one of the civil-disobedience people – defiance campaign leaders who're going to walk into some native location forbidden to Europeans. Next Tuesday. So she'll land herself in prison again. For Christ's sake, Joyce, what are you drinking that stuff for? I've told you that punch is the cheapest muck possible—'

But the girl was not listening to him any longer. Balanced delicately on her rather full, long neck, her fragile-looking face with the fine, short line of nose of a Marie Laurençin painting was looking across the room with the intensity peculiar to the blank-faced. Hers was an essentially two-dimensional prettiness: flat, dazzlingly pastel-coloured, as if the mask of make-up on

41

the unlined skin *were* the face; if one had turned her around, one would scarcely have been surprised to discover canvas. All her life she had suffered from this impression she made of not being quite real.

'She *looks* so nice,' she said now, her eyes still fixed on some point near the door. 'I mean she uses good perfume, and everything. You can't imagine it.'

Her brother-in-law made as if to take the tumbler of alcohol out of the girl's hand, impatiently, the way one might take a pair of scissors from a child, but, without looking at him or at her hands, she changed the glass from one hand to the other, out of his reach. 'At least the brandy's in a bottle with a recognizable label,' he said peevishly. 'I don't know why you don't stick to that.'

'I wonder if she had to eat the same food as the others', said the girl.

'You'll feel like death tomorrow morning,' he said, 'and Madeline'll blame me. You are an obstinate little devil.'

A tall, untidy young man, whose blond head out-topped all others like a tousled palm tree, approached with a slow, drunken smile and, with exaggerated courtesy, asked Joyce to dance. She unhurriedly drank down what was left in her glass, put the glass carefully on the window sill, and went off with him, her narrow waist upright and correct in his long arm. Her brother-in-law followed her with his eyes, irritatedly, for a moment, then closed them suddenly, whether in boredom or in weariness one could not tell.

The young man was saying to the girl as they danced, 'You haven't left the side of your husband – or whatever he is – all night. What's the idea?'

'My brother-in-law,' she said. 'My sister couldn't come because the child's got a temperature.'

He squeezed her waist; it remained quite firm, like the crisp stem of a flower. 'Do I know your sister?' he asked. Every now and then his drunkenness came over him in a delightful swoon, so that his eyelids dropped heavily and he pretended that he was narrowing them shrewdly.

'Maybe. Madeline McCoy – Madeline Barker now. She's the painter. She's the one who started that arts-and-crafts school for Africans.'

'Oh, yes. Yes, I know', he said. Suddenly, he swung her away from him with one hand, executed a few loose-limbed steps around her, lost her in a collision with another couple, caught her to him again, and, with an affectionate squeeze, brought her up short against the barrier of people who were packed tight as a Rugby scrum around the kitchen table, where the drinks were. He pushed her through the crowd to the table.

'What d'you want, Roy, my boy?' said a little, very black-faced African, gleaming up at them.

'Barberton'll do for me.' The young man pressed a hand on the African's head, grinning.

'Ah, that stuff's no good. Sugar-water. Let me give you a dash of Pineapple. Just like mother makes.'

For a moment, the girl wondered if any of the bottles really did contain Pineapple or Barberton, two infamous brews invented by Africans living in the segregated slums that are called locations. Pineapple, she knew, was made out of the fermented fruit and was supposed to be extraordinarily intoxicating; she had once read a newspaper report of a shebeen raid in which the Barberton still contained a lopped-off human foot – whether for additional flavour or the spice of witchcraft, it was not known.

But she was reassured at once. 'Don't worry', said a good-looking blonde, made up to look heavily sun-tanned, who was standing at the bar. 'No shebeen ever produced anything much more poisonous than this gin-punch thing of Derek's.' The host was attending to the needs of his guests at the bar, and she waved at him a glass containing the mixture that the girl had been drinking over at the window.

'Not gin. It's arak – lovely', said Derek. 'What'll you have, Joyce?'

'Joyce', said the gangling young man with whom she had been dancing. 'Joyce. That's a nice name for her. Now tell her mine.'

'Roy Wilson. But you seem to know each other quite adequately without names', said Derek. 'This is Joyce McCoy, Roy – and, Joyce, these are Matt Shabalala, Brenda Shotley, Mahinder Singh, Martin Mathlongo.'

They smiled at the girl: the shiny-faced African, on a level with her shoulder; the blonde woman with the caked powder cracking on her cheeks; the handsome, scholarly-looking Indian with the

43

high, bald dome; the ugly light-coloured man, just light enough for freckles to show thickly on his fleshy face.

She said to her host, 'I'll have the same again, Derek. Your punch.' And even before she had sipped the stuff, she felt a warmth expand and soften inside her, and she said the names over silently to herself – Matt Sha-ba-lala, Martin Math-longo, Ma-hinder Singh. Out of the corner of her eye, as she stood there, she could just see Jessica Malherbe, a short, plump white woman in an elegant black frock, her hair glossy, like a bird's wing, as she turned her head under the light while she talked.

Then it happened, just when the girl was most ready for it, just when the time had come. The little African named Matt said, 'This is Miss Joyce McCoy – Eddie Ntwala', and stood looking on with a smile while her hand went into the slim hand of a tall, light-skinned African with the tired, appraising, cynical eyes of a man who drinks too much in order to deaden the pain of his intelligence. She could tell from the way little Shabalala presented the man that he must be someone important and admired, a leader of some sort, whose every idiosyncrasy – the broken remains of handsome, smoke-darkened teeth when he smiled, the wrinkled tie hanging askew – bespoke to those who knew him his distinction in a thousand different situations. She smiled as if to say, 'Of course, Eddie Ntwala himself, I knew it', and their hands parted and dropped.

The man did not seem to be looking at her – did not seem to be looking at the crowd or at Shabalala, either. There was a slight smile around his mouth, a public smile that would do for anybody. 'Dance?' he said, tapping her lightly on the shoulder. They turned to the floor together.

Eddie Ntwala danced well and unthinkingly, if without much variation. Joyce's right hand was in his left, his right hand on the concavity of her back, just as if – well, just as if he were anyone else. And it was the first time – the first time in all her twenty-two years. Her head came just to the point of his lapel, and she could smell the faint odour of cigarette smoke in the cloth. When he turned his head and her head was in the path of his breath, there was the familiar smell of wine or brandy breathed down upon her by men at dances. He looked, of course, apart from his eyes – eyes that she had seen in other faces and wondered if she would ever be old enough to understand – exactly like any errand 'boy' or house 'boy'. He had the same close-cut wool on his head, the same smooth brown skin, the same rather nice high cheekbones, the same broad-nostrilled small nose. Only, he had his arm around her and her hand in his and he was leading her through the conventional arabesques of polite dancing. She would not let herself formulate the words in her brain: I am dancing with a black man. But she allowed herself to question, with the careful detachment of scientific inquiry, quietly inside herself: 'Do I feel anything? What do I feel?' The man began to hum a snatch of the tune to which they were dancing, the way a person will do when he suddenly hears music out of some forgotten phase of his youth; while the hum reverberated through his chest, she slid her eyes almost painfully to the right, not moving her head, to see his very well-shaped hand – an almost feminine hand compared to the hands of most white men – dark brown against her own white one, the dark thumb and the pale one crossed, the dark fingers and the pale ones folded together. 'Is this exactly how I always dance?' she asked herself closely. 'Do I always hold my back exactly like this, do I relax just this much, hold myself in reserve to just this degree?'

She found she was dancing as she always danced.

I feel nothing, she thought. *I feel nothing.*

And all at once a relief, a mild elation, took possession of her, so that she could begin to talk to the man with whom she was dancing. In any case, she was not a girl who had much small talk; she knew that at least half the young men who, attracted by her exceptional prettiness, flocked to ask her to dance at parties never asked her again because they could not stand her vast minutes of silence. But now she said in her flat, small voice the few things she could say – remarks about the music and the pleasantness of the rainy night outside. He smiled at her with bored tolerance, plainly not listening to what she said. Then he said, as if to compensate for his inattention, 'You from England?'

She said, 'Yes. But I'm not English. I'm South African, but I've spent the last five years in England. I've only been back in South Africa since December. I used to know Derek when I was a little girl', she added, feeling that she was obliged to explain her presence in what she suddenly felt was a group conscious of some distinction or privilege.

'England', he said, smiling down past her rather than at her. 'Never been so happy anywhere.'

'London?' she said.

He nodded. 'Oh, I agree,' she said. 'I feel the same about it.'

'No, you don't, McCoy,' he said very slowly, smiling at her now. 'No, you don't.'

She was silenced at what instantly seemed her temerity.

He said, as they danced around again, 'The way you speak. Really English. Whites in S.A. can't speak that way.'

For a moment, one of the old, blank, impassively pretty-faced silences threatened to settle upon her, but the second glass of arak punch broke through it, and, almost animated, she answered lightly, 'Oh, I find I'm like a parrot. I pick up the accent of the people among whom I live in a matter of hours.'

He threw back his head and laughed, showing the gaps in his teeth. 'How will you speak tomorrow, McCoy?' he said, holding her back from him and shaking with laughter, his eyes swimming. 'Oh, how will you speak tomorrow, I wonder?'

She said, immensely daring, though it came out in her usual small, unassertive feminine voice, a voice gently toned for the utterance of banal pleasantries, 'Like you'.

'Let's have a drink', he said, as if he had known her a long time – as if she were someone like Jessica Malherbe. And he took her back to the bar, leading her by the hand; she walked with her hand loosely swinging in his, just as she had done with young men at country-club dances. 'I promised to have one with Rajati,' he was saying, 'Where has he got to?'

'Is that the one I met?' said the girl. 'The one with the high, bald head?'

'An Indian?' he said. 'No, you mean Mahinder. This one's his cousin, Jessica Malherbe's husband.'

'She's married to an Indian?' The girl stopped dead in the middle of the dancers. 'Is she?' The idea went through her like a thrill. She felt startled as if by a sudden piece of good news about someone who was important to her. Jessica Malherbe – the name, the idea – seemed to have been circling about her life since before she left England. Even there, she had read about her in the papers: the daughter of a humble Afrikaner farmer, who had disowned her in the name of a stern Calvinist God for her anti-nationalism and her radical views; a girl from a back-veld farm – such a farm as Joyce herself could remember seeing from a car window as a child – who had worked in a factory and educated herself and been sent by her trade union to study labour problems all over the world; a girl who negotiated with ministers of state; who, Joyce had learned that evening, had gone to prison for her principles. Jessica Malherbe, who was almost the first person the girl had met when she came in to the party this evening, and who turned out to look like any well-groomed English woman you might see in a London restaurant, wearing a pearl necklace and smelling of expensive perfume. An Indian! It was the final gesture. Magnificent. A world toppled with it – Jessica Malherbe's father's world. An Indian!

'Old Rajati', Ntwala was saying. But they could not find him. The girl thought of the handsome, scholarly-looking Indian with the domed head, and suddenly she remembered that once, in Durban, she had talked across the counter of a shop with an Indian boy. She had been down in the Indian quarter with her sister, and they had entered a shop to buy a piece of silk. She had been the spokeswoman, and she had murmured across the counter to the boy and he had said, in a voice as low and gentle as her own, no, he was sorry, that length of silk was for a sari, and could not be cut. The boy had very beautiful, unseeing eyes, and it was as if they spoke to each other in a dream. The shop was small and deep-set. It smelled strongly of incense, the smell of the village church in which her grandfather had lain in state before his funeral, the scent of her mother's garden on a summer night – the smell of death and flowers, compounded, as the incident itself came to be, of ugliness and beauty, of attraction and repulsion. For just after she and her sister had left the little shop, they had found themselves being followed by an unpleasant man, whose presence first made them uneasily hold tightly to their handbags but who later, when they entered a busy shop in an attempt to get rid of him, crowded up against them and made an obscene advance. He had had a vaguely Eurasian face, they believed, but they could not have said whether or not he was an Indian; in their disgust, he had scarcely seemed human to them at all.

She tried now, in the swarming noise of Derek's room, to hear again in her head the voice of the boy saying the words she

47

remembered so exactly: 'No, I am sorry, that length of silk is for a sari, it cannot be cut.' But the tingle of the alcohol that she had been feeling in her hands for quite a long time became a kind of sizzling in her ears, like the sound of bubbles rising in aerated water, and all that she could convey to herself was the curious finality of the phrase: *can-not-be-cut, can-not-be-cut.*

She danced the next dance with Derek. 'You look sweet tonight, old thing,' he said, putting wet lips to her ear. 'Sweet'.

She said, 'Derek, which is Rajati?'

He let go her waist. 'Over there', he said, but in an instant he clutched her again and was whirling her around and she saw only Mahinder Singh and Martin Mathlongo, the big, freckled coloured man, and the back of some man's dark neck with a businessman's thick roll of fat above the collar.

'Which?' she said, but this time he gestured towards a group in which there were white men only, and so she gave up.

The dance was cut short with a sudden wailing screech as someone lifted the needle of the gramophone in the middle of the record, and it appeared that a man was about to speak. It turned out that it was to be a song and not a speech, for Martin Mathlongo, little Shabalala, two coloured women, and a huge African woman with cork-soled green shoes grouped themselves with their arms hanging about one another's necks. When the room had quietened down, they sang. They sang with extraordinary beauty, the men's voices deep and tender, the women's high and passionate. They sang in some Bantu language, and when the song was done, the girl asked Eddie Ntwala, next to whom she found herself standing, what they had been singing about. He said as simply as a peasant, as if he had never danced with her, exchanging sophisticated banter, 'It's about a young man who passes and sees a girl working in her father's field.'

Roy Wilson giggled and gave him a comradely punch on the arm. 'Eddie's never seen a field in his life. Born and bred in Apex Location.'

Then Martin Mathlongo, with his spotted bow tie under his big, loose-mouthed, strong face, suddenly stood forward and began to sing 'Ol' Man River'. There was something insulting, defiant, yet shamefully supplicating in the way he sang the melodramatic, servile words, the way he kneeled and put out his big hands with

48

their upturned pinkish palms. The dark faces in the room watched him, grinning as if at the antics of a monkey. The white faces looked drunk and withdrawn.

Joyce McCoy saw that, for the first time since she had been introduced to her that evening, she was near Jessica Malherbe. The girl was feeling a strong distress at the sight of the coloured man singing the 'blackface' song, and when she saw Jessica Malherbe, she put – with a look, as it were – all this burden at the woman's feet. She put it all upon her, as if *she* could make it right, for on the woman's broad, neatly made-up face there was neither the sullen embarrassment of the other white faces nor the leering self-laceration of the black.

The girl felt the way she usually felt when she was about to cry, but this time it was the prelude to something different. She made her way with difficulty, for her legs were the drunkest part of her, murmuring politely, 'Excuse me', as she had been taught to do for twenty-two years, past all the people who stood, in their liquor daze, stolid as cows in a stream. She went up to the trade-union leader, the veteran of political imprisonment, the glossy-haired woman who used good perfume. 'Miss Malherbe', she said, and her blank, exquisite face might have been requesting an invitation to a garden party. 'Please, Miss Malherbe, I want to go with you next week. I want to march into the location.'

Next day, when Joyce was sober, she still wanted to go. As her brother-in-law had predicted, she felt sick from Derek's punch, and every time she inclined her head, a great, heavy ball seemed to roll slowly from one side to the other inside her skull. The presence of this ball, which sometimes felt as if it were her brain itself, shrunken and hardened, rattling like a dried nut in its shell, made it difficult to concentrate, yet the thought that she would march into the location the following week was perfectly clear. As a matter of fact, it was almost obsessively clear.

She went to see Miss Malherbe at the headquarters of the Civil Disobedience Campaign, in order to say again what she had said the night before. Miss Malherbe did again just what *she* had done the night before – listened politely, was interested and sympathetic, thanked the girl, and then gently explained that the movement could not allow anyone but bona-fide members to take part in such actions. 'Then I'll become a member now', said Joyce. She wore today a linen dress as pale as her own skin, and on the square of bare, matching flesh at her neck hung a little necklace of small pearls – the sort of necklace that is given to a girl child and added to, pearl by pearl, a new one on every birthday. Well, said Miss Malherbe, she could join the movement, by all means – and would not that be enough? Her support would be much appreciated. But no, Joyce wanted to *do* something; she wanted to march with the others into the location. And before she left the office, she was formally enrolled.

When she had been a member for two days, she went to the head-quarters to see Jessica Malherbe again. This time, there were other people present; they smiled at her when she came in, as if they already had heard about her. Miss Malherbe explained to her the gravity of what she wanted to do. Did she realize that she might have to go to prison? Did she understand that it was the policy of the passive resisters to serve their prison sentences rather than to pay fines? Even if she did not mind for herself, what about her parents, her relatives? The girl said that she was over twenty-one; her only parent, her mother, was in England; she was responsible to no one.

She told her sister Madeline and her brother-in-law nothing. When Tuesday morning came, it was damp and cool. Joyce dressed with the consciousness of the performance of the ordinary that marks extraordinary days. Her stomach felt hollow; her hands were cold. She rode into town with her brother-in-law, and all the way his car popped the fallen jacaranda flowers, which were as thick on the street beneath the tyres as they were on the trees. After lunch, she took a tram to Fordsburg, a quarter where Indians and people of mixed blood, debarred from living any-where better, lived alongside poor whites, and where, it had been decided, the defiers were to foregather. She had never been to this part of Johannesburg before, and she had the address of the house to which she was to go written in her tartan-silk-covered notebook in her minute, backward-sloping hand. She carried her white angora jacket over her arm and she had put on sensible flat sandals. I don't know why I keep thinking of this as if it were a lengthy expedition, requiring some sort of special equipment, she thought;

actually it'll be all over in half an hour. Jessica Malherbe said we'd pay bail and be back in town by four-thirty.

The girl sat in the tram and did not look at the other passengers, and they did not look at her, although the contrast between her and them was startling. They were thin, yellow-limbed children with enormous sooty eyes; bleary-eyed, shuffling men, whom degeneracy had enfeebled into an appearance of indeterminate old age; heavy women with swollen legs, who were carrying newspaper parcels; young, almost white factory girls whose dull, kinky hair was pinned up into a decent simulation of fashionable style, and on whose proud, pert faces rouge and lipstick had drawn a white girl's face.

She got off at the stop she had been told to and went slowly up the street, watching the numbers. It was difficult to find out how far she would have to walk, or even, for the first few minutes, whether she was walking in the right direction, because the numbers on the doorways were half obliterated, or ill-painted, or sometimes missing entirely. As in most poor quarters, houses and stores were mixed, and, in fact, some houses were being used as business premises, and some stores had rooms above, in which, obviously, the storekeepers and their families lived. The street had a flower name, but there were no trees and no gardens. Most of the shops had Indian firm names amateurishly written on home-made wooden signboards or curlicued and flourished in signwriter's yellow and red across the lintel: Moonsammy Dadoo, Hardware, Ladies Smart Outfitting & General; K. P. Patel & Sons, Fruit Merchants; Vallabhir's Bargain Store. A shoemaker had enclosed the veranda of his small house as a workshop, and had hung outside a huge black tin shoe, of a style worn in the Twenties.

The gutters smelled of rotting fruit. Thin *café-au-lait* children trailed smaller brothers and sisters; on the veranda of one of the little semi-detached houses a lean light-coloured man in shirt sleeves was shouting, in Afrikaans, at a fat woman who sat on the steps. An Indian woman in a sari and high-heeled European shoes was knocking at the door of the other half of the house. Farther on, a very small house, almost eclipsed by the tentacles of voracious-looking creepers, bore a polished brass plate with the name and consulting hours of a well-known Indian doctor.

The street was quiet enough; it had the dead, listless air of all

51

places where people are making some sort of living in a small way. And so Joyce started when a sudden shriek of drunken laughter came from behind a rusty corrugated-iron wall that seemed to enclose a yard. Outside the wall, someone was sitting on a patch of the tough gritty grass that sometimes scrabbles a hold for itself on worn city pavements; as the girl passed, she saw that the person was one of the white women tramps whom she occasionally saw in the city crossing a street with the peculiar glassy purposefulness of the outcast.

She felt neither pity nor distaste at the sight. It was as if, dating from this day, her involvement in action against social injustice had purged her of sentimentality; she did not have to avert her gaze. She looked quite calmly at the woman's bare legs, which were tanned, with dirt and exposure, to the colour of leather. She felt only, in a detached way, a prim, angry sympathy for the young pale-brown girl who stood nursing a baby at the gate of the house just beyond, because she had to live next door to what was almost certainly a shebeen.

Then, ahead of her in the next block, she saw three cars parked outside a house and knew that that must be the place. She walked a little faster, but quite evenly, and when she reached it – No. 260, as she had been told – she found that it was a small house of purplish brick, with four steps leading from the pavement to the narrow veranda. A sword fern in a paraffin tin, painted green, stood on each side of the front door, which had been left ajar, as the front door sometimes is in a house where there is a party. She went up the steps firmly, over the dusty imprints of other feet, and, leaning into the doorway a little, knocked on the fancy glass panel of the upper part of the door. She found herself looking straight down a passage that had a worn flowered linoleum on the floor. The head of a small Indian girl – low forehead and great eyes – appeared in a curtained archway half-way down the passage and disappeared again instantly.

Joyce McCoy knocked again. She could hear voices, and, above all the others, the tone of protest in a woman's voice.

A bald white man with thick glasses crossed the passage with quick, nervous steps and did not, she thought, see her. But he might have, because, prompted perhaps by his entry into the room from which the voices came, the pretty brunette woman with the efficient manner, whom the girl remembered from the party, appeared suddenly with her hand outstretched and said enthusiastically, 'Come *in*, my dear. Come inside. Such a racket in there! You could have been knocking all day.'

The girl saw that the woman wore flimsy sandals and no stockings, and that her toenails were painted like the toes of the languid girls in *Vogue*. The girl did not know why details such as these intrigued her so much, or seemed so remarkable. She smiled in greeting and followed the woman into the house.

Now she was really there; she heard her own footsteps taking her down the passage of a house in Fordsburg. There was a faintly spicy smell about the passage; on the wall she caught a glimpse of what appeared to be a photograph of an Indian girl in European bridal dress, the picture framed with fretted gold paper, like a cake frill. And then they were in a room where everyone smiled at her quickly but took no notice of her. Jessica Malherbe was there, in a blue linen suit, smoking a cigarette and saying something to the tall, tousle-headed Roy Wilson, who was writing down what she said. The bald man was talking low and earnestly to a slim woman who wore a man's wrist-watch and had the hands of a man. The tiny African, Shabalala, wearing a pair of spectacles with thin tortoise-shell rims, was ticking a pencilled list. Three or four others, black and white, sat talking. The room was as brisk with chatter as a birds' cage.

Joyce lowered herself gingerly onto a dining-room chair whose legs were loose and swayed a little. And as she tried to conceal herself and sink into the composition of the room, she noticed a group sitting a little apart, near the windows, in the shadow of the heavy curtains, and, from the arresting sight of them, saw the whole room as it was beneath the overlay of people. The group was made up of an old Indian woman, and a slim Indian boy and another Indian child, who were obviously her grandchildren. The woman sat with her feet apart, so that her lap, under the voluminous swathings of her sari, was broad, and in one nostril a ruby twinkled. Her hands were little and beringed – a fat woman's hands. Her forehead was low beneath the coarse black hair and the line of tinsel along the sari, and she looked out through the company of white men and women, Indian men in business suits, Africans in clerkly neatness, as if she were deaf or could not see. Yet when Joyce saw her eyes move, as cold and as lacking in interest as the eyes of a tortoise, and her foot stir, asserting an inert force of life, like the twitch in a muscle of some supine creature on a mud-bank, the girl knew it was not deafness or blindness that kept the woman oblivious of the company but simply the knowledge that this house, this room, was her place. She was here before the visitors came; she would not move for them; she would be here when they had gone. And the children clung with their grand-mother, knowing that she was the kind who could never be banished to the kitchen or some other backwater.

From the assertion of this silent group the girl became aware of the whole room (*their* room), of its furnishings: the hideous 'suite' upholstered in imitation velvet with a stamped design of triangles and sickles; the yellow varnished table with the pink silk mat and the brass vase of paper roses; the easy chairs with circular apertures in the arms where coloured glass ash trays were balanced; the crudely coloured photographs; the barbola vase; the green ruched-silk cushions; the standard lamp with more platforms for more coloured glass ash trays; the gilded plaster dog that stood at the door. An Indian went over and said something to the old woman with the proprietary, apologetic, irritated air of a son who wishes his mother would keep out of the way; as he turned his head, the girl saw something familiar in the angle and recognized him as the man the back of whose neck she had seen when she was trying to identify Jessica Malherbe's husband at the party. Now he came over to her, a squat, pleasant man, with a great deal of that shiny black Indian hair making his head look too big for his body. He said, 'My congratulations. My wife, Jessica, tells me you have insisted on identifying yourself with today's defiance. Well, how do you feel about it?'

She smiled at him with great difficulty; she really did not know why it was so difficult. She said, 'I'm sorry. We didn't meet that night. Just your cousin – I believe it is? – Mr. Singh.' He was such a remarkably commonplace-looking Indian, Jessica Malherbe's husband, but Jessica Malherbe's husband after all – the man with the roll of fat at the back of his neck.

She said, 'You don't resemble Mr. Singh in the least', feeling that it was herself she offended by the obvious thought behind the comparison, and not this fat, amiable middle-aged man, who needed only to be in his shirt sleeves to look like any well-to-do

54

Indian merchant, or in a grubby white coat, and unshaven, to look like a fruit-and-vegetable hawker. He sat down beside her (she could see the head of the old woman just beyond his ear), and as he began to talk to her in his Cambridge-modulated voice, she began to notice something that she had not noticed before. It was curious, because surely it must have been there all the time; then again it might not have been – it might have been released by some movement of the group of the grandmother, the slender boy, and the child, perhaps from their clothes – but quite suddenly she began to be aware of the odour of incense. Sweet and dry and smoky, like the odour of burning leaves – she began to smell it. Then she thought, It must be in the furniture, the curtains; the old woman burns it and it permeates the house and all the gewgaws from Birmingham, and Denver, Colorado, and American-occupied Japan. Then it did not remind her of burning leaves any longer. It was incense, strong and sweet. The smell of death and flowers. She remembered it with such immediacy that it came back literally, absolutely, the way a memory of words or vision never can.

'Are you all right, Miss McCoy?' said the kindly Indian, interrupting himself because he saw that she was not listening and that her pretty, pale, impassive face was so white and withdrawn that she looked as if she might faint.

She stood up with a start that was like an inarticulate apology and went quickly from the room. She ran down the passage and opened a door and closed it behind her, but the odour was there, too, stronger than ever, in somebody's bedroom, where a big double bed had an orange silk cover. She leaned with her back against the door, breathing it in and trembling with fear and with the terrible desire to be safe: to be safe from one of the kindly women who would come, any moment now, to see what was wrong; to be safe from the gathering up of her own nerve to face the journey in the car to the location, and the faces of her companions, who were not afraid, and the walk up the location street.

The very conventions of the life which, she felt, had insulated her in softness against the sharp, joyful brush of real life in action came up to save her now. If she was afraid, she was also polite. She had been polite so long that the colourless formula of good manners, which had stifled so much spontaneity in her, could also serve to stifle fear.

It would be so *terribly rude* simply to run away out of the house, and go home, now.

That was the thought that saved her – the code of a well-brought-up child at a party – and it came to her again and again, slowing down her thudding heart, uncurling her clenched hands. *It would be terribly rude to run away now.* She knew with distress, somewhere at the back of her mind, that this was the wrong reason for staying, but it worked. Her manners had been with her longer and were stronger than her fear. Slowly the room ceased to sing so loudly about her, the bedspread stopped dancing up and down before her eyes, and she went slowly over to the mirror in the door of the wardrobe and straightened the belt of her dress, not meeting her own eyes. Then she opened the door and went down the passage and back again into the room where the others were gathered, and sat down in the chair she had left. It was only then that she noticed that the others were standing – had risen, ready to go.

'What about your jacket, my dear. Would you like to leave it?' the pretty brunette said, noticing her.

Jessica Malherbe was on her way to the door. She smiled at Joyce and said, 'I'd leave it, if I were you.'

'Yes, I think so, thank you.' She heard her own voice as if it were someone else's.

Outside, there was the mild confusion of deciding who should go with whom and in which car. The girl found herself in the back of the car in which Jessica Malherbe sat beside the driver. The slim, mannish woman got in; little Shabalala got in but was summoned to another car by an urgently waving hand. He got out again, and then came back and jumped in just as they were off. He was the only one who seemed excited. He sat forward, with his hands on his knees. Smiling widely at the girl, he said, 'Now we really are taking you for a ride, Miss McCoy.'

The cars drove through Fordsburg and skirted the city. Then they went out one of the main roads that connect the goldmining towns of the Witwatersrand with each other and with Johannesburg. They passed mine dumps, pale grey and yellow; clusters of neat, ugly houses, provided for white mineworkers; patches of veld, where the rain of the night before glittered thinly in low places; a brickfield; a foundry; a little poultry farm. And then they turned in to a muddy road, along which they followed a bus that swayed under its load of passengers, exhaust pipe sputtering black smoke, canvas flaps over the windows wildly agitated. The bus thundered ahead through the location gates, but the three cars stopped outside. Jessica Malherbe got out first, and stood, pushing back the cuticles of the nails of her left hand as she talked in a businesslike fashion to Roy Wilson. 'Of course, don't give the statement to the papers unless they ask for it. It would be more interesting to see *their* version first, and come along with our own afterwards. But they *may* ask—'

'There's a press car,' Shabalala said, hurrying up. 'There.'

'Looks like Brand, from the *Post.*'

'Can't be Dick Brand; he's transferred to Bloemfontein', said the tall, mannish woman.

'Come here, Miss McCoy, you're the baby', said Shabalala, straightening his tie and twitching his shoulders, in case there was going to be a photograph. Obediently, the girl moved to the front.

But the press photographer waved his flash bulb in protest. 'No, I want you walking.'

'Well, you better get us before we enter the gates or you'll find yourself arrested, too', said Jessica Malherbe, unconcerned. 'Look at that', she added to the mannish woman, lifting her foot to show the heel of her white shoe, muddy already.

Lagersdorp Location, which they were entering and which Joyce McCoy had never seen before, was much like all such places. A high barbed-wire fence – more a symbol than a means of confinement, since, except for the part near the gates, it had comfortable gaps in many places – enclosed almost a square mile of dreary little dwellings, to which the African population of the near-by town came home to sleep at night. There were mean houses and squalid tin shelters and, near the gates where the administrative offices were, one or two decent cottages, which had been built by the white housing authorities 'experimentally' and never duplicated; they were occupied by the favourite African clerks of the white location superintendent. There were very few shops, since every licence granted to a 'native' shop in a location takes business away from the white stores in the town, and there were a great many churches, some built of mud and tin, some neo-Gothic and built of brick, representing a great many sects.

They began to walk, the seven men and women, towards the

location gates. Jessica Malherbe and Roy Wilson were a little ahead, and the girl found herself between Shabalala and the bald white man with thick glasses. The flash bulb made its brief sensation, and the two or three picannins who were playing with tin hoops on the roadside looked up, astonished. A fat black woman selling oranges and roast mealies shouted speculatively to a passer-by in ragged trousers.

At the gateway, a fat black policeman sat on a soapbox and gossiped. He raised his hand to his cap as they passed. In Joyce McCoy, the numbness that had followed her nervous crisis began to be replaced by a calm embarrassment; as a child she had often wondered, seeing a circle of Salvation Army people playing a hymn out of tune on a street corner, how it would feel to stand there with them. Now she felt she knew. Little Shabalala ran a finger around the inside of his collar, and the girl thought, with a start of warmth, that he was feeling as she was; she did not know that he was thinking what he had promised himself he would not think about during this walk – that very likely the walk would cost him his job. People did not want to employ Africans who 'made trouble'. His wife, who was immensely proud of his education and his cleverness, had said nothing when she learned that he was going – had only gone, with studied consciousness, about her cooking. But, after all, Shabalala, like the girl – though neither he nor she could know it – was also saved by convention. In his case, it was a bold convention – that he was an amusing little man. He said to her as they began to walk up the road, inside the gateway, 'Feel the bump?'

'I beg your pardon?' she said, polite and conspiratorial.

A group of ragged children, their eyes alight with the tenacious beggarliness associated with the East rather than with Africa, were jumping and running around the white members of the party, which they thought was some committee come to judge a competition for the cleanest house, or a baby show. 'Penny, *missus*, penny, penny, *baas*!' they whined. Shabalala growled something at them playfully in their own language before he answered, with his delightful grin, wide as a slice of melon. 'The bump over the colour bar.'

Apart from the children, who dropped away desultorily, like flying fish behind a boat, no one took much notice of the defiers.

The African women, carrying on their heads food they had bought in town, or bundles of white people's washing, scarcely looked at them. African men on bicycles rode past, preoccupied. But when the party came up parallel with the administration offices – built of red brick, and, along with the experimental cottages at the gate and the clinic next door, the only buildings of European standard in the location – a middle-aged white man in a suit worn shiny on the seat and the elbows (his slightly stooping body seemed to carry the shape of his office chair and desk) came out and stopped Jessica Malherbe. Obediently, the whole group stopped; there was an air of quiet obstinacy about them. The man, who was the location superintendent himself, evidently knew Jessica Malherbe, and was awkward with the necessity of making this an official and not a personal encounter. 'You know that I must tell you it is prohibited for Europeans to enter Lagersdorp Location', he said. The girl noticed that he carried his glasses in his left hand, dangling by one earpiece, as if he had been waiting for the arrival of the party and had jumped up from his desk nervously at last.

Jessica Malherbe smiled, and there was in her smile something of the easy, informal amusement with which Afrikaners discount pomposity. 'Mr. Dougal, good afternoon. Yes, of course, we know you have to give us official warning. How far do you think we'll get?'

The man's face relaxed. He shrugged and said, 'They're waiting for you.'

And suddenly the girl, Joyce McCoy, felt this – the sense of something lying in wait for them. The neat, stereotyped faces of African clerks appeared at the windows of the administrative offices. As the party approached the clinic, the European doctor in his white coat looked out; two white nurses and an African nurse came out onto the veranda. And all the patient African women who were sitting about in the sun outside, suckling their babies and gossiping, sat silent while the party walked by – sat silent, and had in their eyes something of the look of the Indian grandmother, waiting at home in Fordsburg.

The party walked on up the street, and on either side, in the little houses, which had home-made verandas flanking the strip of worn, unpaved earth that was the sidewalk, or whose front doors

59

opened straight out on to a foot or two of fenced garden where hens ran and pumpkins had been put to ripen, doors were open, and men and women stood, their children gathered in around them, as if they sensed the approach of a storm. Yet the sun was hot on the heads of the party, walking slowly up the street. And they were silent, and the watchers were silent, or spoke to one another only in whispers, each bending his head to another's ear but keeping his eyes on the group passing up the street. Someone laughed, but it was only a drunk – a wizened little old man – returning from some shebeen. And ahead at the corner of a crossroad stood the police car, a black car, with the aerial from its radio-communication equipment a shining lash against all the shabbiness of the street. The rear doors opened, and two heavy, smartly dressed policemen got out and slammed the doors behind them. They approached the party slowly, not hurrying themselves. When they drew abreast, one said, as if in reflex, 'Ah – good afternoon'. But the other cut in, in an emotionless official voice, 'You are all under arrest for illegal entry into Lagersdorp Location. If you'll just give us your names . . .'

Joyce stood waiting her turn and her heart beat slowly and evenly. She thought again, as she had once before – how long ago was that party? – I feel *nothing*. It's all right. I feel *nothing*.

But as the policeman came to her, and she spelled out her name for him, she looked up and saw the faces of the African onlookers who stood nearest her. Two men, a small boy, and a woman, dressed in ill-matched cast-offs of European clothing, which hung upon them without meaning, like coats spread on bushes, were looking at her. When she looked back, they met her gaze. And she felt, suddenly, not *nothing* but what they were feeling at the sight of her, a white girl, taken – incomprehensibly, as they themselves were used to being taken – under the force of white men's wills, which dispensed and withdrew life, which imprisoned and set free, fed or starved, like God himself.

The Bridegroom

He came into his road camp that afternoon for the last time. It was neater than any house would ever be; the sand raked smooth in the clearing, the water drums under the tarpaulin, the flaps of his tent closed against the heat. Thirty yards away a black woman knelt, pounding mealies, and two or three children, grey with Kalahari dust, played with a skinny dog. Their shrillness was no more than a bird's piping in the great spaces in which the camp was lost.

Inside his tent, something of the chill of the night before always remained, stale but cool, like the air of a church. There was his iron bed, with its clean pillowcase and big kaross. There was his table, his folding chair with the red canvas seat, and the chest in which his clothes were put away. Standing on the chest was the alarm clock that woke him at five every morning and the photograph of the seventeen-year-old girl from Francistown whom he was going to marry. They had been there a long time, the girl and the alarm clock; in the morning when he opened his eyes, in the afternoon when he came off the job. But now this was the last time. He was leaving for Francistown in the Roads Department ten-tonner, in the morning; when he came back, the next week, he would be married and he would have with him the girl, and the caravan which the department provided for married men. He had his eye on her as he sat down on the bed and took off his boots; the smiling girl was like one of those faces cut out of a magazine. He began to shed his working overalls, a rind of khaki stiff with dust that held his shape as he discarded it, and he called, easily and softly, '*Ou Piet, ek wag.*' But the bony black man with his eyebrows raised like a clown's, in effort, and his bare feet shuffling under the weight, was already at the tent with a tin bath in which hot water made a twanging tune as it slopped from side to side.

When he had washed and put on a clean khaki shirt and a pair of worn grey trousers, and streaked back his hair with sweet-smelling pomade, he stepped out of his tent just as the lid of the horizon closed on the bloody eye of the sun. It was winter and the sun set shortly after five; the grey sand turned a fading pink, the low thorn scrub gave out spreading stains of lilac shadow that presently all ran together; then the surface of the desert showed pocked and pored, for a minute or two, like the surface of the moon through a telescope, while the sky remained light over the darkened earth and the clean crystal pebble of the evening star shone. The campfires – his own and the black men's, over there – changed from near-invisible flickers of liquid colour to brilliant focuses of leaping tongues of light; it was dark. Every evening he sat like this through the short ceremony of the closing of the day, slowly filling his pipe, slowly easing his back round to the fire, yawning off the stiffness of his labour. Suddenly he gave a smothered giggle, to himself, of excitement. Her existence became real to him; he saw the face of the photograph, posed against a caravan door. He got up and began to pace about the camp, alert to promise. He kicked a log farther into the fire, he called an order to Piet, he walked up towards the tent and then changed his mind and strolled away again. In their own encampment at the edge of his, the road gang had taken up the exchange of laughing, talking, yelling, and arguing that never failed them when their work was done. Black arms gestured under a thick foam of white soap, there was a gasp and splutter as a head broke the cold force of a bucketful of water, the gleaming bellies of iron cooking pots were carried here and there in the talkative preparation of food. He did not understand much of what they were saying – he knew just enough Tswana to give them his orders, with help from Piet and one or two others who understood his own tongue, Afrikaans – but the sound of their voices belonged to this time of evening. One of the babies who always cried was keeping up a thin, ignored wail; the naked children were playing the chasing game that made the dog bark. He came back and sat down again at the fire, to finish his pipe.

After a certain interval (it was exact, though it was not timed by a watch, but by long habit that had established the appropriate

62

lapse of time between his bath, his pipe, and his food) he called out, in Afrikaans, 'Have you forgotten my dinner, man?'

From across the patch of distorted darkness where the light of the two fires did not meet, but flung wobbling shapes and opaque, overlapping radiances, came the hoarse, protesting laugh that was, better than the tribute to a new joke, the pleasure in constancy to an old one.

Then a few minutes later: 'Piet! I suppose you've burned everything, eh?'

'*Baas?*'

'Where's the food, man?'

In his own time the black man appeared with the folding table and an oil lamp. He went back and forth between the dark and light, bringing pots and dishes and food, and nagging with deep satisfaction, in a mixture of English and Afrikaans. 'You want *koeksusters*, so I make *koeksusters*. You ask me this morning. So I got to make the oil nice and hot, I got to get everything ready . . . It's a little bit slow. Yes, I know. But I can't get everything quick, quick. You hurry tonight, you don't want wait, then it's better you have *koeksusters* on Saturday, then I'm got time in the afternoon, I do it nice . . . Yes, I think next time it's better . . .'

Piet was a good cook. 'I've taught my boy how to make everything', the young man always told people, back in Francistown. 'He can even make *koeksusters*', he had told the girl's mother, in one of those silences of the woman's disapproval that it was so difficult to fill. He had had a hard time, trying to overcome the prejudice of the girl's parents against the sort of life he could offer her. He had managed to convince them that the life was not impossible, and they had given their consent to the marriage, but they still felt that the life was unsuitable, and his desire to please and reassure them had made him anxious to see it with their eyes and so forestall, by changes, their objections. The girl was a farm girl, and would not pine for town life, but, at the same time, he could not deny to her parents that living on a farm with her family around her, and neighbours only thirty or forty miles away, would be very different from living two hundred and twenty miles from a town or village, alone with him in a road camp 'surrounded by a gang of kaffirs all day', as her mother had said. He himself simply did not think at all about what the girl would do while he

63

was out on the road; and as for the girl, until it was over, nothing could exist for her but the wedding, with her two little sisters in pink walking behind her, and her dress that she didn't recognize herself in, being made at the dressmaker's, and the cake that was ordered with a tiny china bride and groom in evening dress, on the top.

He looked at the scored table, and the rim of the open jam tin, and the salt cellar with a piece of brown paper tied neatly over the broken top, and said to Piet, 'You must do everything nice when the missus comes.'

'*Baas?*'

They looked at each other and it was not really necessary to say anything.

'You must make the table properly and do everything clean.'

'Always I make everything clean. Why you say now I must make clean—'

The young man bent his head over his food, dismissing him.

While he ate his mind went automatically over the changes that would have to be made for the girl. He was not used to visualizing situations, but to dealing with what existed. It was like a lesson learned by rote; he knew the totality of what was needed, but if he found himself confronted by one of the component details, he foundered: he did not recognize it or know how to deal with it. The boys must keep out of the way. That was the main thing. Piet would have to come to the caravan quite a lot, to cook and clean. The boys – especially the boys who were responsible for the main-tenance of the lorries and road-making equipment – were always coming with questions, what to do about this and that. They'd mess things up, otherwise. He spat out a piece of gristle he could not swallow; his mind went to something else. The women over there – they could do the washing for the girl. They were such a raw bunch of kaffirs, would they ever be able to do anything right? Twenty boys and about five of their women – you couldn't hide them under a thorn bush. They just mustn't hang around, that's all. They must just understand that they mustn't hang around. He looked round keenly through the shadow-puppets of the half-dark on the margin of his fire's light; the voices, companionably quieter, now, intermittent over food, the echoing *chut!* of wood being chopped, the thin film of a baby's wail through which all these sounded – they were on their own side. Yet he felt an odd, rankling suspicion.

His thoughts shuttled, as he ate, in a slow and painstaking way that he had never experienced before in his life – he was worrying. He sucked on a tooth; Piet, Piet, that kaffir talks such a hell of a lot. How's Piet going to stop talking, talking every time he comes near? If he talks to her . . . Man, it's sure he'll talk to her. He thought, in actual words, what he would say to Piet about this; the words were like those unsayable things that people write on walls for others to see in private moments, but that are never spoken in their mouths.

Piet brought coffee and *koeksusters* and the young man did not look at him.

But the *koeksusters* were delicious, crisp, sticky, and sweet, and as he felt the familiar substance and taste on his tongue, alternating with the hot bite of the coffee, he at once became occupied with the pure happiness of eating as a child is fully occupied with a bag of sweets. *Koeksusters* never failed to give him this innocent, total pleasure. When first he had taken the job of overseer to the road gang, he had had strange, restless hours at night and on Sundays. It seemed that he was hungry. He ate but never felt satisfied. He walked about all the time, like a hungry creature. One Sunday he actually set out to walk (the Roads Department was very strict about the use of the ten-tonner for private purposes) the fourteen miles across the sand to the cattle-dipping post where the government cattle officer and his wife, Afrikaners like himself and the only other white people between the road camp and Francistown, lived in their corrugated-iron house. By a coincidence, they had decided to drive over and see him, that day, and they had met him a little less than halfway, when he was already slowed and dazed by heat. But shortly after that Piet had taken over the cooking of his meals and the care of his person, and Piet had even learned to make *koeksusters*, according to instructions given to the young man by the cattle officer's wife. The *koeksusters*, a childhood treat that he could indulge in whenever he liked, seemed to mark his settling down; the solitary camp became a personal way of life, with its own special arrangements and indulgences.

'*Ou Piet! Kèrel!* What did you do to the *koeksusters*, hey?' he called out joyously.

A shout came that meant 'Right away'. The black man

appeared, drying his hands on a rag, with the diffident, kidding manner of someone who knows he has excelled himself.

'Whatsa matter with the *koeksusters*, man?'

Piet shrugged. 'You must tell me. I don't know what's matter.'

'Here, bring me some more, man.' The young man shoved the empty plate at him, with a grin. And as the other went off, laughing, the young man called. 'You must always make them like that, see?'

He liked to drink at celebrations, at weddings or Christmas, but he wasn't a man who drank his brandy every day. He would have two brandies on a Saturday afternoon, when the week's work was over, and for the rest of the time, the bottle that he brought from Francistown when he went to collect stores lay in the chest in his tent. But on this last night he got up from the fire on impulse and went over to the tent to fetch the bottle (one thing he didn't do, he didn't expect a kaffir to handle his drink for him; it was too much of a temptation to put in their way). He brought a glass with him, too, one of a set of six made of tinted imitation cut glass, and he poured himself a tot and stretched out his legs where he could feel the warmth of the fire through the soles of his boots. The nights were not cold, until the wind came up at two or three in the morning, but there was a clarifying chill to the air; now and then a figure came over from the black men's camp to put another log on the fire whose flames had dropped and become blue. The young man felt inside himself a similar low incandescence; he poured himself another brandy. The long yelping of the jackals prowled the sky without, like the wind about a house; there was no house, but the sounds beyond the light his fire tremblingly inflated into the dark – that jumble of meaningless voices, crying babies, coughs, and hawking – had built walls to enclose and a roof to shelter. He was exposed, turning naked to space on the sphere of the world as the speck that is a fly plastered on the window of an aeroplane, but he was not aware of it.

The lilt of various kinds of small music began and died in the dark; threads of notes, blown and plucked, that disappeared under the voices. Presently a huge man whose thick black body had strained apart every seam in his ragged pants and shirt loped silently into the light and dropped just within it, not too near the fire. His feet, intimately crossed, were cracked and weathered like driftwood. He held to his mouth a one-stringed instrument shaped like a lyre, made out of a half-moon of bent wood with a ribbon of dried palm leaf tied from tip to tip. His big lips rested gently on the strip and while he blew, his one hand, by controlling the vibration of the palm leaf, made of his breath a small, faint, perfect music. It was caught by the very limits of the capacity of the human ear; it was almost out of range. The first music men ever heard, when they began to stand upright among the rushes at the river, might have been like it. When it died away it was difficult to notice at what point it really had gone.

'Play that other one', said the young man, in Tswana. Only the smoke from his pipe moved.

The pink-palmed hands settled down round the instrument. The thick, tender lips were wet once. The faint desolate voice spoke again, so lonely a music that it came to the player and listener as if they heard it inside themselves. This time the player took a short stick in his other hand and, while he blew, scratched it back and forth inside the curve of the lyre, where the notches cut there produced a dry, shaking, slithering sound, like the far-off movement of dancers' feet. There were two or three figures with more substance than the shadows, where the firelight merged with the darkness. They came and squatted. One of them had half a paraffin tin, with a wooden neck and other attachments of gut and wire. When the lyre-player paused, lowering his piece of stick and leaf slowly, in ebb, from his mouth, and wiping his lips on the back of his hand, the other began to play. It was a thrumming, repetitive, banjo tune. The young man's boot patted the sand in time to it and he took it up with hand-claps once or twice. A thin, yellowish man in an old hat pushed his way to the front past sarcastic remarks and twittings and sat on his haunches with a little clay bowl between his feet. Over its mouth there was a keyboard of metal tongues. After some exchange, he played it and the others sang low and nasally, bringing a few more strollers to the fire. The music came to an end, pleasantly, and started up again, like a breath drawn. In one of the intervals the young man said, 'Let's have a look at that contraption of yours, isn't it a new one?' and the man to whom he signalled did not understand what was being said to him but handed over his paraffin-tin mandolin with pride and also with amusement at his own handiwork.

The young man turned it over, twanged it once, grinning and shaking his head. Two bits of string and an old jam tin and they'll make a whole band, man. He'd heard them playing some crazy-looking things. The circle of faces watched him with pleasure; they laughed and lazily remarked to each other; it was a funny-looking thing, all right, but it worked. The owner took it back and played it, clowning a little. The audience laughed and joked appreciatively; they were sitting close in to the fire now, painted by it. 'Next week' the young man raised his voice gaily – 'next week when I come back, I bring radio with me, plenty real music. All the big white bands play over it—' Someone who had once worked in Johannesburg said, 'Satchmo', and the others took it up, understanding that this was the word for what the white man was going to bring from town. Satchmo. Satch-mo. They tried it out, politely. 'Music, just like at a big white dance in town. Next week.' A friendly, appreciative silence fell, with them all resting back in the warmth of the fire and looking at him indulgently. A strange thing happened to him. He felt hot, over first his neck, then his ears and his face. It didn't matter, of course; by next week they would have forgotten. They wouldn't expect it. He shut down his mind on a picture of them, hanging round the caravan to listen, and him coming out on the steps to tell them—

He thought for a moment that he would give them the rest of the bottle of brandy. Hell, no, man, it was mad. If they got the taste for the stuff, they'd be pinching it all the time. He'd give Piet some sugar and yeast and things from the stores, for them to make beer tomorrow when he was gone. He put his hands deep in his pockets and stretched out to the fire with his head sunk on his chest. The lyre-player picked up his flimsy piece of wood again, and slowly what the young man was feeling inside himself seemed to find a voice; up into the night beyond the fire, it went, uncoiling from his breast and bringing ease. As if it had been made audible out of infinity and could be returned to infinity at any point, the lonely voice of the lyre went on and on. Nobody spoke, the barriers of tongues fell with silence. The whole dirty tide of worry and planning had gone out of the young man. The small, high moon, outshone by a spiky spread of cold stars, repeated the shape of the lyre. He sat for he was not aware how long, just as he had for so many other nights, with the stars at his head and the fire at his feet.

But at last the music stopped and time began again. There was tonight; there was tomorrow, when he was going to drive to Francistown. He stood up; the company fragmented. The lyre-player blew his nose into his fingers. Dusty feet took their accustomed weight. They went off to their tents and he went off to his. Faint plangencies followed them. The young man gave a loud, ugly, animal yawn, the sort of unashamed personal noise a man can make when he lives alone. He walked very slowly across the sand; it was dark but he knew the way more surely than with his eyes. 'Piet! Hey!' he bawled as he reached his tent. 'You get up early tomorrow, eh? And I don't want to hear the lorry won't start. You get it going and then you call me. D'you hear?'

He was lighting the oil lamp that Piet had left ready on the chest and as it came up softly it brought the whole interior of the tent with it: the chest, the bed, the clock, and the coy smiling face of the seventeen-year-old girl. He sat down on the bed, sliding his palms through the silky fur of the kaross. He drew a breath and held it for a moment, looking round purposefully. And then he picked up the photograph, folded the cardboard support back flat to the frame, and put it in the chest with all his other things, ready for the journey.

The African Magician

*S*hips always assemble the same cast, and this one was no exception. The passengers were not, of course, the ones you would meet on any of those liners described as floating hotels that take tourists to and fro between places where they never stay long enough to see the bad season come. But, as if supplied by some theatrical agency unmindful of a change of style in the roles available in the world, these passengers setting off up the Congo River instead of across an ocean were those you might have met at any time as long as the colonial era lasted, travelling between the country in Europe where they were born, and the country across the sea where its flag also flew. The time was two months before the Belgian Congo became Zaire. There was the old hand who inevitably trapped my husband by the hour; released at last, he would come to me deeply under the man's deadly fascination. '. . . twenty-two years . . . prospecting for minerals for the government . . . torpedoed going back to Belgium in the war . . . Free French . . . two and a half years in a Russian prison camp . . . he still carries his card signed by de Gaulle . . .'

'Oh I know, I know, I don't want to see it.'

But when the old hand interrupted his evening stroll round the deck to sit down where we sat, outside our cabin, no measure of aloofness, head bent to book, would prevent him from cornering my eye at some point and growling with a pally wink, 'Two more years and I sit and drink beer and look at the girls in Brussels. Best beer, best girls in the world.' When he saw us, leaning together over the rail but lost from each other and ourselves in the sight of the towering, indifferent fecundity of the wilderness that the river cleaved from height to depth, he would pause, hang about, and then thrust the observation between our heads – 'Lot of bloomin' nothing, eh? Country full of nothing. Bush, bush, trees, trees. Put you two metres in there and you won't come out never.' His mind ran down towards some constant, smug yet uncertain vision of his retirement, that must have been with him all the twenty-two years. 'Bush, nothing.'

There were sanitary officers, a police officer, a motor mechanic, agricultural officers, and research workers, returning with their wives and children from home leave in Belgium. The women looked as if they had been carved out of lard, and were in the various stages of reproduction – about to give birth, or looking after small fat children who might have been believed to be in danger of melting. There was a priest who sat among the women in the row of deck-chairs all day, reading paperbacks; he was a big elderly man with a forward-thrust, intelligent jaw, and when he stood up slowly and leant upon the rail, his hard belly lifting his cassock gave him the sudden appearance of an odd affinity with the women around him. There was a newly married couple, of course – that look of a pair tied up for a three-legged race who haven't mastered the gait yet. The husband was ordinary enough but the girl was unexpected, among the browsing herd setting to over the first meal aboard. She was very tall, the same size as her husband, and her long thin naked legs in shorts showed the tense tendon, fleshless, on each inner thigh as she walked. On the extreme thinness and elongation of the rest of her – half pathetic, half elegant – was balanced a very wide square jaw. In profile the face was pretty; full on, the extraordinary width of her blemished forehead, her thick black eyebrows above grey eyes, her very big straight mouth with pale lips, was a distortion of unusual beauty. Her style could have been Vogue model, or beatnik. In fact she was a Belgian country girl who had hit naturally, by an accident of physique and a natural sluttishness, upon what I knew only as a statement of artifice of one kind or another.

The boat, broad and tiered top-heavy upon the water like a Mississippi paddle steamer, had powerful Diesel engines beating in her flat floor, and we pushed two barges covered with cars, jeeps, and tanks of beer, and another passenger boat, painted drab but soon fluttering with the flags of the third class's washing. There was a lot of life going on down there at the other boat; you could look down the length of the two barges from the deck in front of our cabin and see it – barbering, cooking, a continual swarming and clambering from deck to deck that often overflowed on to the barges. Jars of palm wine passed between our galley and crew's quarters, and their galley. A tin basin full of manioc spinach appeared at intervals moving along in the air from the bowels of the boat beneath our feet; then we saw the straight, easygoing body of the black beauty on whose turban it was balanced. She went down the street of the barges with langour; winding easily between the tethered cars, stopping to disparage a basket of dried fish that had just been dumped aboard from a visiting canoe, or to parry some flattering and insulting suggestion from a member of the crew lounging off duty, and finally disappeared into the boat at the other end.

The police officer's wife noticed a scribble chalked on the barge below us. 'My God, take a look at that, will you!' It did not consist, as messages publicly addressed to no one in particular usually do, of curses or declarations of love, but hailed, in misspelt French and the uneven script of some loiterer in Léopoldville harbour, the coming of the country's independence of white man's rule. 'They are mad, truly. They think they can run a country.' She was a gay one, strongly made-up, with a small waist and wide jelly-hips in bright skirts, and she had the kind of roving alertness that put her on chatting terms with the whole boat within twenty-four hours. In case I had missed the point, she turned to me and said in English, 'They are just like monkeys, you know. We've taught them a few tricks. Really, they are monkeys out from *there*.' And she gestured at the forest that we were passing before night and day, while we looked and while we slept.

Our passengers were all white, not because of a colour bar, but because even those few black people who could afford the first class thought it a waste of money. Yet except for the Belgian captain, who never came down among us from his quarters on the top deck, the entire crew was black, and we were kept fed and clean by a small band of Congolese men. They managed this with an almost mysterious ease. There were only three stewards and a barman visible, and often, five minutes before the bell rang for a meal, I would see them sitting on their haunches on the barge below us, barefoot and in dirty shorts, murmuring their perpetual tide of gossip. But however promptly you presented yourself at table, they

72

were there before you, in mildewed white cotton suits and forage caps decorated with the shipping company's badge. Only their bare feet provided a link with the idlers of a few minutes before. The idlers never looked up and did not notice a greeting from the decks above them; but the stewards were grinning and persuasive, pressing food on you, running to get your wine with a happy, speedy slither that implied a joking reference to your thirst. When we stopped at river stations and the great refrigerated hold was opened, we recognized the same three, grunting as they tossed the weight of half a frozen ox from hand to hand; once I remarked to George, who waited on us and even took it upon himself to wake us in time for breakfast, pounding on our cabin door and calling 'Chop! Chop!' – 'You were working hard this afternoon, eh?'

But he looked at me blankly. 'Madam?'

'Yes, unloading. I saw you unloading meat.'

'It wasn't me', he said.

'Not you, in the green shirt?'

He shook his head vehemently. It appeared as if I had insulted him by the suggestion. And yet it was he, all right, his gruff laugh and small moustache and splayed toes. 'No, no, not me.' Wasn't it a known fact that to white people all black faces look alike? How could I argue with him?

In the evenings the priest put on grey flannel trousers and smoked a big cigar; you would have said then that he was a big businessman, successful and yet retaining some residue of sensitivity in the form of sadness – my husband found out that he was in fact the financial administrator of a remote and very large complex of mission schools. I was often aware of him, without actually seeing him, when I was in our cabin at night: he liked to stand alone on the deserted bend of the deck, outside. The honeymoon couple (as we thought of the newly married pair, although their honeymoon was over and he was taking her to the inland administrative post where he worked) formed the habit of coming there too, during the hot hours when everyone was resting after lunch. He, with his fair curly hair and rather snouty, good-looking face, would stand looking out at the leap and glitter of the water, but she could see nothing but him, he was blown up to fill the screen of her vision, and in this exaggerated projection, every detail, every hair and pore held her attention like the features of a landscape.

Fascinated, she concentrated on squeezing blackheads from his chin. I used to come noisily out of the cabin, hoping to drive this idyll away. But they were not aware of me; she was not aware of the presence of another woman, like herself, recognizing the ugliness of some intimacies when seen, as they never should be, as a spectator. 'Why must they choose our deck?' I was indignant.

My husband was amused. 'Come on, what's the matter with love?' He lay on his bed grinning, picking at a tooth with a match.

'That's not love. I wouldn't mind nearly so much if I found them copulating on the deck.'

'Oh wouldn't you? That's because you never have.'

The thing was that I could not help expecting something of that face – the girl's face. As I have said, it was not a fraud in the ways that it might have been – a matter of fashion in faces or ideas. She had come by it honestly, so to speak, and I could not believe that it was not the outward sign of some remarkable quality, not, perhaps, an obvious one, like a talent, but some bony honesty of mind or freshness of spirit. It disappointed me to see that face, surfeit as a baby's bleary with milk with the simplest relationship with a commonplace man. I was reluctant to admit that her intensity at table was merely a ruthless desire to get the choice bits of every dish shovelled on to his plate. I felt irritated when I came upon her, sitting placidly cobbling the torn ribbon of a vulgar frilly petticoat made of rainbow-coloured net: it was simply a face, that was all, clapped on the same old bundle of well-conformed instincts and the same few feelings. Yet every time I saw it I could not suppress a twinge of hopeful disbelief; this was part of the mild preoccupation with a collection of lives you will never touch on again, that, because it is entirely gratuitous, makes a voyage so restful.

Our first stop was in the middle of the night, and next morning we woke up to find the ivory sellers aboard. They came from the forest and the expressions on their faces were made difficult to read by distracting patterns of tattooing, but they wore white cotton vests from a trading store. Out of cardboard school cases they spread ivory toothpicks, paper-knives, and bracelets on the narrow deck, and squatted among them. Nearly all the Belgians had seen this tourist bric-à-brac many times before, but they gathered round, asking prices challengingly, and then putting the stuff down and walking away. A few women, sheepish about it, bought bracelets, and shook them on their wrists as if deciding they were not so bad, after all. One of the agricultural officers, whose child, learning to walk, hampered his father's left leg like a manacle, said, 'Have you locked your door? You want to, while these fellows are about. They'll take anything.'

The vendor outside our cabin hadn't taken anything, but I don't think he had sold anything, either. Just before lunchtime he packed his cardboard case again and went off down to the public thoroughfare of the barges, where a pirogue was tied, trailing alongside in the water like a narrow floating leaf. He did not seem downcast; but then, as I have remarked, it was difficult to tell, with those rows of nicks running in curved lines across his forehead, and the sharp cuts tightening the skin under the eyes.

People brought all sorts of things aboard to sell, and they were all sorts of people, too, for we were following the river a thousand miles through the homes of many tribes. Sometimes old hags with breasts like bellpulls and children with dusty bellies sprang up on the dark river-bank and yelled "*depen*DANCE!' The young men and girls of the same village would swim out ahead of our convoy, and drift past us with darting, uplifted eyes, begging for jam tins from the galley. Those men who managed to scramble aboard, to our eyes dressed in their sleek wet blackness, hid their penises between their closed thighs with exactly that instinct that must have come to Adam when he was cast out of the Garden. The gesture put them, although they lived alone in the forest among the wild creatures, apart from the animal life they shared, just as it had done to him, for himself and them, forever.

The pirogues came with live turtles, and with fish, with cloudy beer and wine made from bananas, palm nuts, or sorghum, and with the smoked meat of hippopotamus and crocodile. The vendors did a good trade with our crew and the passengers down at the third-class boat; the laughter, the exclamations, and the argument of bargaining were with us all day, heard but not understood, like voices in the next room. At stopping places, the people who were nourished on these ingredients of a witches' brew poured ashore across the single plank flung down for them, very human in contour, the flesh of the children sweet, the men and women strong and sometimes handsome. We, thank God, were fed on veal and ham and Brussels sprouts, brought frozen from Europe.

When our convoy put off some contribution to the shore instead of taking on some of its fruits, the contribution was usually something outlandish and bulky. A product of heavy industry, some chunk of machinery or road-making tractor, set down in a country that has not been industrialized, looks as strange as a space-ship from Mars might, set down in a city. A strip of landing-stage with a tin shed, a hut or two, not quite African and not quite a white man's house, a row of empty oil drums, and a crane, standing like some monster water-bird on three legs above the water: the crane came into action with the rattle of chains playing out, and there, hanging in the air ready to land where its like had never been seen, where, in fact, there was nothing that could prepare one for the look of it, were the immense steel angles of something gleaming with grey paint and intricate with dials where red arrows quivered. Cars and jeeps went ashore this way, too, dangling, but they seemed more agile, adaptable, and accepted, and no sooner were they ashore than some missionary or trader jumped in, and they went scrambling away up the bank and disappeared.

We stopped, one day, long enough for us to be able to go ashore and wander round a bit; it was quite a place – white provincial offices in a garden with marigolds on a newly cleared space of raw red earth, a glass and steel hospital in the latest contemporary architecture, an avenue of old palms along the waterfront leading to a weathered red brick cathedral. And when the taxi we had hired drove a mile out along the single road that led away into the forest, all this was hidden by the forest as if already it were one of those ancient lost cities that are sometimes found in a rich humus grave, dead under the rotting green, teeming culture of life. Another day, we stopped only long enough for us to go ashore but stay within sight of the boat. There was nothing much to see; it was Sunday, and a few Portuguese traders and their fat wives in flowered dresses were sitting on the veranda of a house, drinking lemonade; opposite, a tin store sold sewing machines and cigarettes. A crumbling white fort, streaked with livid moss and being pushed apart by the swelling roots of trees like the muscles of Samson, remained from the days eighty years ago when the Arab slave-traders built it. The African village that they had raided and burned, incidentally providing a convenient place for the fort, had left no trace except, perhaps, the beginning of the line of continuity that leads men always to build where others, enemies or vanished, have lived before them.

Someone came aboard at this brief stopping-place, just as, at the stop in the ivory country behind us, the ivory vendors had.

At dinner that evening we found slips of paper with a typewritten announcement on our tables. There was to be an entertainment, at 8 p.m., in the bar. Gentlemen, 80 francs, Ladies, 70 francs. There was a stir of amusement in the dining-room. I thought, for a moment, of a Donkey Derby or Bingo game. My husband said, 'A choir, I'll bet. Girls singing mission-school hymns. They must have been practising down at the other boat.'

'What's this?' I asked George.

'You will like it', he said.

'But what is it, a show or what?'

'Very good,' he said. 'You will see. A man who does things you have never seen. Very clever.' When we had finished eating the sweet course he came skidding back to hit at our swiftly cleared table with a napkin, scattering crumbs. 'You are coming in the bar?' – he made sure. It was a kindly but firm command. We began to have that obscure anxiousness to see the thing a success that descends upon one at school concerts and amateur theatricals. Oh yes, we were coming, all right. We usually took coffee on deck, but this time we carried our cups straight into the lounge, where the bar occupied one wall and the fans in the low panelled ceiling did not dispel the trapped heat of the day, but blew down upon the leather chairs a perpetual emanation of radio music coming from loudspeakers set in grilles overhead. We were almost the first there; we thought we might as well take good seats at one of the tables right in front of the space that had been cleared before the bar. The senior administrator and his daughter, who sat in the bar every night playing tric-trac, got up and went out. There were perhaps fourteen or fifteen of us, including the honeymoon couple, who had looked in several times, grinning vaguely, and at last had decided to come. 'What a lot of mean bastards, eh?' said my husband admiringly. It did seem a surprising restraint that could resist an unspecified local entertainment offered in the middle of a green nowhere. The barman, a handsome young Bacongo from Léopoldville, leaned an elbow on the counter and stared at us. George came in from the dining-room and bent his head to talk closely to him; he remained, hunched against the counter, smiling at the room with the reassuring, confident smile that the compère sends out into the proscenium whether it is addressed to faces set close as a growth of pinhead mould, or a blankness of empty seats.

At last, the entertainment began. It was, of course, a magician, as we had understood from George it must be. The man walked in suddenly from the deck – perhaps he had been waiting there behind the stacked deck-chairs for the right moment. He wore a white shirt and grey trousers and carried an attaché case. He had an assistant with him, a very black, dreamy squat chap, most likely picked up as a volunteer from among the passengers down at the third-class boat. He spent most of the performance sitting astride a chair with his chin on his arms on the high back.

There was a hesitant spatter of clapping as the magician came in, but he did not acknowledge it and it quickly died out. He went to business at once; out of the attaché case, that was rather untidily filled, came bits of white paper, scissors, a bunch of paper flowers, and strings of crumpled flags. His first trick was a card trick, an old one that most of us had seen many times before, and one or two of us could have done himself. There were a few giggles and only one person attempted to clap; but the magician had already gone on to his next illusion, which involved the string of pennants and a hat. Then there was the egg that emerged from his ear. Then the fifty-franc note that was torn up before our eyes and made whole again, not exactly before them, but almost.

Between each item of his performance there was an interval when he turned his back protectively to us and made some preparation hidden beneath a length of black cloth. Once he spoke to the barman, and was given a glass. He did not seem to be aware of the significance of applause when he got it, and he went through his revelations without a word of patter, not even the universally understood exclamations, like *Abracadabra!*, or *Hey presto!* gestures without which it is impossible to imagine a magician bringing anything off. He did not smile and we saw his small filed white teeth in his smooth black face only when his upper lip lifted in concentration; his eyes, though they met ours openly, were inner-focused. He went through what was clearly his limited repertoire, learned God knows where or from whom (perhaps even by some extraordinary correspondence course?), without mishap, but only just. When he crunched up the glass and ate it, for instance, he did not wear the look of eye-rolling agony that is this trick's professional accompaniment, and makes even the most sceptical audience hold its breath in sympathy – he looked fearful and anxious, his face twitching like the face of someone crawling through a barbed-wire fence. After half an hour he turned away at the conclusion of a trick and began folding up the string of flags, and we assumed that there would now be an interval before the second part of the performance. But at once the assistant got up from his chair and came round the room with a plate, preceded by George, who handed out all over again the slips of paper that we had found on our tables at dinner: *An entertainment, 8 p.m., in the bar. Gentlemen, 80 francs, Ladies, 70 francs.* The performance was over. The audience, who had felt flat anyway, felt done down. One of the Belgian ladies demurred, smiling, 'Seventy francs for this!'

Tomorrow morning, at ten o'clock, George announced proudly to each table, there would be a repeat performance, same prices for adults, 30 francs for children. We could all see the magician again then.

'It's too much, too expensive.' One of the Belgians spoke up for us all. 'You can't charge eighty francs for only half an hour. Is this all he knows?'

There were murmurs of half-interested assent; some people were inclined to go off to bed, anyway. The objection was explained to George, and his organizer's pride died slowly, wonderingly, out of his manner. Suddenly he waggled a reassuring palm of the hand; it would be all right, he would make it all right, and his idiotic assurance, based on what, we could not imagine – eventual return of our money? another performance, free? – was so sweeping that everybody handed over their 70 and 80 francs doggedly, as a condition he expected us to fulfil.

Then he went to the magician and began to talk to him in a low, fast, serious voice, not without a tinge of scorn and exasperation, whether directed towards the magician or towards us we did not know, because none of us understood the language being spoken.

The barman leaned over to hear and the assistant stood stolidly in the little huddle.

Only two members of the audience had gone to bed, after all; the rest of us sat there, amused, but with a certain thread of tension livening us up. It was clear that most of the people did not like to be done down, it was a matter they prided themselves on – not to be done down, even by blacks, whom they didn't expect to have the same standards about these things and whom they thought of as thievish anyway. Our attitude – that of my husband and myself – was secretly different, though the difference could not show outwardly. Tempted though we were to treat the whole evening as a joke and a rather naïve extortion of 150 francs from our pockets, we had the priggish feeling that it was perhaps patronizing and a kind of insult to make special allowances for these people, simply because they were black. If they chose, as they had, to enter into activity governed by Western values, whether it was conjuring or running a twentieth-century state, they must be done the justice of being expected to fulfil their chosen standards. For the sake of the magician himself and our relation to him as an audience, he must himself give us his 150 francs' worth. We finished our glasses of beer (we had picked up the habit) while the urgent discussion between George, the barman, and the magician went on.

The magician seemed adamant. Almost before George had begun to speak, he was shaking his head, and he did not stop packing away the stuff of his illusions – the cards, the paper flowers, the egg. He drew his lips back from his teeth and answered in the hard tone of flat refusal, again and again. But George and the barman closed in on him verbally, a stream of words that flowed round and spilled over challenges. Quite suddenly the magician gave in, must have given in, on what sounded like a disclaimer of all responsibility, a warning and a reluctant submission more in the nature of a challenge itself.

George turned to us with a happy grin. He bowed and threw up his hands. 'I have told him too short. Now he makes some more for you. Some magic.' And he laughed, lifting his eyebrows and inclining his head so that his white forage cap nearly fell off, implying that the whole business was simply a miracle to him, as it must be to us.

The magician bowed too. And we clapped him; it was sporting, on both sides. The newly married girl rested her head a moment on the snouty young man's shoulder, and yawned in his ear. Then we were all attention. The assistant, who had taken the opportunity to subside into his chair again, was summoned by the magician and made to stand before him. Then the magician ran a hand along inside the waistband of his trousers, tucking in his shirt in a brief, final, and somehow preparatory gesture, and began to make passes with his hands in front of the assistant's face. The assistant blinked, like a sleepy dog worried by a fly. His was a dense, coaly face, bunched towards the front with a strong jutting jaw, puffy lips, and a broad nose with a single tattoo mark like a line of ink drawn down it. He had long, woolly eyelashes and they seemed to sway over his eyes. The magician's black hands were thin and the yellow-pink palms looked almost translucent; he might not have had the words, but he had the gestures, all right, and his hands curled like serpents and fluttered like birds. The assistant began to dance. He shuffled away from the magician, the length of the bar, the slither and hesitation from one foot to another, neck retracted and arms bent at elbows like a runner, that Africans can do as soon as they learn to walk, and that they can always do, drunk or sober, even when they are so old that they can scarcely walk. A subdued but generous laughter went up. We were all ready to give the magician good-natured encouragement, now that he was trying. The magician continued to stand, his hands fallen now at his sides, his slim body modest and relaxed, hanging from his shoulders in its shabby clean shirt and too-big grey trousers. He kept his eyes quietly on the assistant, and the man turned and came back to him, singing now as well as dancing, and in a young *girl's* voice. And here we all laughed without any prompting wish to seem appreciative. As a hypnotist the magician had the sense of timing that he lacked so conspicuously when performing tricks, and before the laughter stopped he had said something curtly to the assistant, and the man went over to the bar counter and picking up an empty glass jug that stood there, drank it off in deep, gasping gulps as if he had been wandering for days in a desert. He was returned to his inanimate self by one movement of the magician's hands before his face; he looked at us all without surprise, and then, finding himself the focus of an attention that did not even arouse him to any curiosity, sat down in his chair again and yawned.

'Let's see what he can do with someone else, not his own man!' one of the Belgians called out good-humouredly, signalling for the barman at the same time. 'Yes, come on, someone else. Ask him to try someone he doesn't know.'

'You want it, yes?' George was grinning. He pointed a finger at the magician.

'You, George, let's see if he can do you!'

'No, one of *us*'. A shiny, tubby-faced man in cocoa research, who had towards the blacks the chaffing, half-scornful ease of one of those who knew them well, swung round in his chair. 'That's an idea, eh? Let him have a go at one of us, and see how he gets on.' 'Yes, yes'. There was a positive chorus of rising assent; even the honeymooners joined in. Someone said, 'But what about the language? How can he suggest things in our minds if we don't know the same language?' – but she was dismissed, and George explained to the magician what was wanted.

He made no protest; in a swift movement he walked away towards the bar a few steps and then turned to face us, at bay. I noticed that his nostrils – he had a fine nose – moved in and out once or twice as if he were taking slow deep breaths.

We were waiting, I suppose, for him to call upon one of us, one of the men, of course – the cocoa man and some others were ready for the right moment. a rough equivalent of the familiar: Will any kind gentleman or lady please step up onto the stage? But oddly it did not come. Over the giggles and nudges and half-sentences, an expectancy fell. We sat looking at the awkward young black man, searching slowly along our faces, and we did not know when the performance had begun. Fidgeting died out, looking at him, and our eyes surrounded him closely. He was still as any prey run to ground. And then while we were looking at him, waiting for him to choose one of us, we became aware of a sudden smooth movement in our ranks. My attention was distracted to the right, and I saw the girl – the honeymoon girl, my girl with the face – get up with a little exclamation, a faint wondering *tst!* . . . of remembering something, and walk calmly, without brushing against anything, over to the magician. She stood directly before him, quite still, her tall rounded shoulders drooping naturally and thrusting forward a little her head, that was raised to him, almost on a level with his own. He did not move; he did not gaze; his eyes blinked quietly. She put up her long arms and, standing just their length from him, brought her hands to rest on his shoulders. Her cropped head dropped before him to her chest.

It was the most extraordinary gesture. None of us could see her face; there was nothing but the gesture. God knows where it came from – *he* could not have put it into her will, it was not in any hypnotist's repertoire, and she, surely, could not have had the place for something so *other*, in her female, placidly sensual nature. I don't think I have ever seen such a gesture before, but I knew – they knew – we all knew what it meant. It was nothing to do with what exists between men and women. She had never made such a gesture to her husband, or any man. She had never stood like that before her father – none of us has. How can I explain? One of the disciples might have come before Christ like that. There was the peace of absolute trust in it. It stirred a needle of fear in me – more than that, for a moment I was horribly afraid; and how can I explain that, either? For it was beautiful, and I have lived in Africa all my life and I know them, *us*, the white people. To see it was beautiful would make us dangerous.

The husband sat hunched back in his chair in what was to me a most unexpected reaction – his fist pushed his cheek out of shape and he was frozenly withdrawn, like a parent witnessing a suddenly volunteered performance by a child who, so far as he knew, had neither talent nor ambition. But the cocoa expert, who had dealt with the blacks so long, acted quickly, and jumped up calling, authoritative, loud, but only just controlled, 'Hey! No, no, we want him to try his magic with the men, tell him not the ladies. No, no, he must take a man.'

The room was released as if it had struck a blow. And at the same moment the magician, before George had begun to translate sharply at him, understood without understanding words and passed his hand across the lower part of his own face in an almost servile movement that bumped the arms of the girl without deliberately touching her, and released her instantly from the gesture. At once she laughed and was dazed, and as her husband came to her as if to escort an invalid, I heard her saying pleasedly, 'It's wonderful! You should try! Like a dreamy feeling . . . really!'

She had missed the sight of the gesture; she was the only person at ease in the room.

There was no performance next morning. I suppose the first audience had been too disappointingly small. When my husband asked mildly after the magician, at lunch, George said inattentively, 'He has gone.' We had not made a stop anywhere, but of course pirogues were constantly coming and going between us and the shore.

Our boat began to take on the look of striking camp; we were due at Stanleyville in two days, and some of the Belgians were getting off at the big agricultural research station where we would call a few hours before Stanleyville. Tin trunks with neat lettering began to appear outside the cabins. The honeymoon couple spent hours down on the second barge, cleaning their car – they had rags and a bucket, and they let the bucket down into the Congo and then sloshed the brown water over the metal, that was too hot to touch. The old hand changed a tyre on his jeep and announced that he had room for two passengers going from Stanleyville north, towards the Sudan. Only my husband and I and the priest made no preparations; we two had the meagre luggage of air travellers, and the single briefcase of papers for the congress on tropical diseases that we were going to attend, and he was in no hurry to be first off the boat at Stanleyville since, he explained, he would have to wait there several weeks, perhaps, before a car went his way – the mission could not send all that distance specially to fetch him. He had run out of reading matter and allowed himself a cigar in broad daylight as we leaned on the rail together on the morning of our last day aboard, watching passengers struggling ashore from the third-class boat against the stream of visitors and people selling things, coming up the gangplank. We had stopped, with the usual lack of ceremony at such places, at some point in a mile-long village of huts thatched with banana leaves and surrounded by banana plantations that stretched along the river bank. The two boats and the barges stood out in the water at an angle from the shore; the link with it was a tenuous one. But babies and goats and bicycles passed over it, and among them I saw the magician. He looked like any other young black clerk, with his white shirt and grey trousers, and the attaché case. All Africa carries an attaché case now; and what I knew was in that one might not be more extraordinary than what might be in some of the others.

Not for Publication

*I*t is not generally known – and it is never mentioned in the
official biographies – that the Prime Minister spent the first
eleven years of his life, as soon as he could be trusted not to
get under a car, leading his uncle about the streets. His uncle
was not really blind, but nearly, and he was certainly mad. He
walked with his right hand on the boy's left shoulder; they kept
moving part of the day, but they also had a pitch on the cold side
of the street, between the legless man near the post office who sold
bootlaces and copper bracelets, and the one with the doll's hand
growing out of one elbow, whose pitch was outside the YWCA.
That was where Adelaide Graham-Grigg found the boy, and later
he explained to her, 'If you sit in the sun they don't give you
anything.'

Miss Graham-Grigg was not looking for Praise Basetse. She
was in Johannesburg on one of her visits from a British Protectorate, seeing friends, pulling strings, and pursuing, on the side, her
private study of following up the fate of those people of the tribe
who had crossed the border and lost themselves, sometimes over
several generations, in the city. As she felt down through the papers
and letters in her bag to find a sixpence for the old man's hat, she
heard him mumble something to the boy in the tribe's tongue –
which was not in itself anything very significant in this city where
many African languages could be heard. But these sounds formed
in her ear as words: it was the language that she had learnt to
understand a little. She asked, in English, using only the traditional
form of address in the tribe's tongue, whether the old man was a
tribesman. But he was mumbling the blessings that the clink of a
coin started up like a kick to a worn and useless mechanism. The
boy spoke to him, nudged him; he had already learnt in a rough

way to be a businessman. Then the old man protested, no, no, he had come a long time from that tribe. A long, long time. He was Johannesburg. She saw that he confused the question with some routine interrogation at the pass offices, where a man from another territory was always in danger of being endorsed out to some forgotten 'home'. She spoke to the boy, asking him if he came from the Protectorate. He shook his head terrifiedly; once before he had been ordered off the streets by a welfare organization. 'But your father? Your mother?' Miss Graham-Grigg said, smiling. She discovered that the old man had come from the Protectorate, from the very village she had made her own, and that his children had passed on to their children enough of the language for them all to continue to speak it among themselves, down to the second generation born in the alien city.

Now the pair were no longer beggars to be ousted from her conscience by a coin: they were members of the tribe. She found out what township they went to ground in after the day's begging, interviewed the family, established for them the old man's right to a pension in his adopted country, and, above all, did something for the boy. She never succeeded in finding out exactly who he was – she gathered he must have been the illegitimate child of one of the girls in the family, his parentage concealed so that she might go on with her schooling. Anyway, he was a descendant of the tribe, a displaced tribesman, and he could not be left to go on begging in the streets. That was as far as Miss Graham-Grigg's thoughts for him went, in the beginning. Nobody wanted him particularly, and she met with no opposition from the family when she proposed to take him back to the Protectorate and put him to school. He went with her just as he had gone through the streets of Johannesburg each day under the weight of the old man's hand.

The boy had never been to school before. He could not write, but Miss Graham-Grigg was astonished to discover that he could read quite fluently. Sitting beside her in her little car in the khaki shorts and shirt she had bought him, stripped of the protection of his smelly rags and scrubbed bare to her questions, he told her that he had learnt from the newspaper vendor whose pitch was on the corner: from the posters that changed several times a day, and then from the front pages of the newspapers and magazines spread there. Good God, what had he not learnt on the street! Everything from his skin out unfamiliar to him, and even that smelling strangely different – this detachment, she realized, made the child talk as he could never have done when he was himself. Without differentiation, he related the commonplaces of his life; he had also learnt from the legless copper bracelet man how to make *dagga* cigarettes and smoke them for a nice feeling. She asked him what he thought he would have done when he got older, if he had had to keep on walking with his uncle, and he said that he had wanted to belong to one of the gangs of boys, some little older than himself, who were very good at making money. They got money from white people's pockets and handbags without their even knowing it, and if the police came they began to play their penny whistles and sing. She said with a smile, 'Well, you can forget all about the street, now. You don't have to think about it ever again.' And he said, 'Yes, med-dam', and she knew she had no idea what he was thinking – how could she? All she could offer were more unfamiliarities, the unfamiliarities of generalized encouragement, saying, 'And soon you will know how to write.'

She had noticed that he was hatefully ashamed of not being able to write. When he had had to admit it, the face that he turned open and victimized to her every time she spoke had the squinting grimace – teeth showing and a grown-up cut between the faint, child's eyebrows – of profound humiliation. Humiliation terrified Adelaide Graham-Grigg as the spectacle of savage anger terrifies others. That was one of the things she held against the missionaries: how they stressed Christ's submission to humiliation, and so had conditioned the people of Africa to humiliation by the white man.

Praise went to the secular school that Miss Graham-Grigg's committee of friends of the tribe in London had helped pay to set up in the village in opposition to the mission school. The sole qualified teacher was a young man who had received his training in South Africa and now had been brought back to serve his people; but it was a beginning. As Adelaide Graham-Grigg often said to the Chief, shining-eyed as any proud daughter, 'By the time independence comes we'll be free not only of the British government, but of the church as well.' And he always giggled a little embarrassedly, although he knew her so well and was old enough to be her father, because her own father was both a former British MP and the son of a bishop.

It was true that everything was a beginning; that was the beauty of it – of the smooth mud houses, red earth, flies and heat that visitors from England wondered she could bear to live with for months on end, while their palaces and cathedrals and streets choked on a thousand years of used-up endeavour were an ending. Even Praise was a beginning: one day the tribe would be economically strong enough to gather its exiles home, and it would no longer be necessary for its sons to sell their labour over that border. But it soon became clear that Praise was also exceptional. The business of learning to read from newspaper headlines was not merely a piece of gutter wit; it proved to have been the irrepressible urge of real intelligence. In six weeks the boy could write, and from the start he could spell perfectly, while boys of sixteen and eighteen never succeeded in mastering English orthography. His arithmetic was so good that he had to be taught with the Standard Three class instead of the beginners; he grasped at once what a map was; and in his spare time showed a remarkable aptitude for understanding the workings of various mechanisms, from water-pumps to motorcycle engines. In eighteen months he had completed the Standard Five syllabus, only a year behind the average age of a city white child with all the background advantage of a literate home.

There was as yet no other child in the tribe's school who was ready for Standard Six. It was difficult to see what could be done now, but send Praise back over the border to school. So Miss Graham-Grigg decided it would have to be Father Audry. There was nothing else for it. The only alternative was the mission school, those damned Jesuits who'd been sitting in the Protectorate since the days when the white imperialists were on the grab, taking the tribes under their 'protection' – and the children the boy would be in class with there wouldn't provide any sort of stimulation, either. So it would have to be Father Audry, and South Africa. He was a priest, too, an Anglican one, but his school was a place where at least, along with the pious pap, a black child could get an education as good as a white child's.

When Praise came out into the veld with the other boys his eyes screwed up against the size: the land ran away all round, and there was no other side to be seen; only the sudden appearance of the sky, that was even bigger. The wind made him snuff like a dog. He stood helpless as the country men he had seen caught by changing traffic lights in the middle of a street. The bits of space between buildings came together, ballooned uninterruptedly over him, he was lost; but there were clouds as big as the buildings had been, and even though space was vaster than any city, it was peopled by birds. If you ran for ten minutes into the veld the village was gone; but down low on the ground thousands of ants knew their way between their hard mounds that stood up endlessly as the land.

He went to herd cattle with the other boys early in the mornings and after school. He taught them some gambling games they had never heard of. He told them about the city they had never seen. The money in the old man's hat seemed a lot to them, who had never got more than a few pennies when the mail train stopped for water at the halt five miles away; so the sum grew in his own estimation too, and he exaggerated it a bit. In any case, he *was* forgetting about the city, in a way; not Miss Graham-Grigg's way, but in the manner of a child, who makes, like a wasp building with its own spittle, his private context within the circumstance of his surroundings, so that the space around him was reduced to the village, the pan where the cattle were taken to drink, the halt where the train went by; whatever particular patch of sand or rough grass astir with ants the boys rolled on, heads together, among the white egrets and the cattle. He learnt from the others what roots and leaves were good to chew, and how to set wire traps for spring-hares. Though Miss Graham-Grigg had said he need not, he went to church with the children on Sundays.

He did not live where she did, in one of the Chief's houses, but with the family of one of the other boys; but he was at her house often. She asked him to copy letters for her. She cut things out of the newspapers she got and gave them to him to read; they were about aeroplanes, and dams being built, and the way the people lived in other countries. 'Now you'll be able to tell the boys all about the Volta Dam, that is also in Africa – far from here – but still, in Africa,' she said, with that sudden smile that reddened her face. She had a gramophone and she played records for him. Not only music, but people reading out poems, so that he knew that the poems in the school reader were not just short lines of words, but more like songs. She gave him tea with plenty of sugar and she asked him to help her to learn the language of the tribe, to talk to her in it. He was not allowed to call her *madam* or *missus*, as he did the white women who had put money in the hat, but had to learn to say *Miss Graham-Grigg*.

Although he had never known any white women before except as high-heeled shoes passing quickly in the street, he did not think that all white women must be like her; in the light of what he had seen white people, in their cars, their wealth, their distance, to be, he understood nothing that she did. She looked like them, with her blue eyes, blonde hair, and skin that was not one colour but many: brown where the sun burned it, red when she blushed — but she lived here in the Chief's houses, drove him in his car, and sometimes slept out in the fields with the women when they were harvesting kaffircorn far from the village. He did not know why she had brought him there, or why she should be kind to him. But he could not ask her, any more than he would have asked her why she went out and slept in the fields when she had a gramophone and a lovely gas lamp (he had been able to repair it for her) in her room. If, when they were talking together, the talk came anywhere near the pitch outside the post office, she became slowly very red, and they went past it, either by falling silent or (on her part) talking and laughing rather fast.

That was why he was amazed the day she told him that he was going back to Johannesburg. As soon as she had said it she blushed darkly for it, her eyes pleading confusion: so it was really from her that the vision of the pitch outside the post office came again. But she was already speaking: '. . . to school. To a really good boarding school, Father Audry's school, about nine miles from town. You must get your chance at a good school, Praise. We really can't teach you properly any longer. Maybe you'll be the teacher here yourself, one day. There'll be a high school, and you'll be the headmaster.'

She succeeded in making him smile; but she looked sad, uncertain. He went on smiling because he couldn't tell her about the initiation school that he was about to begin with the other boys of his age-group. Perhaps someone would tell her. The other women. Even the Chief. But you couldn't fool her with smiling.

'You'll be sorry to leave Tebedi and Joseph and the rest.'

He stood there, smiling.

'Praise, I don't think you understand about yourself – about your brain.' She gave a little sobbing giggle, prodded at her own head. 'You've got an awfully good one. More in there than other boys – you know? It's something special – it would be such a waste. Lots of people would like to be clever like you, but it's not easy, when you are the clever one.'

He went on smiling. He did not want her face looking into his any more and so he fixed his eyes on her feet, white feet in sandals with the veins standing out over the ankles like the feet of Christ dangling above his head in the church.

Adelaide Graham-Grigg had met Father Audry before, of course. All those white people who do not accept the colour bar in southern Africa seem to know each other, however different the bases of their rejection. She had sat with him on some committee or other in London a few years earlier, along with a couple of exiled white South African leftists and a black nationalist leader. Anyway, everyone knew him – from the newspapers, if nowhere else: he had been warned, in a public speech by the Prime Minister of the South African Republic, Dr. Verwoerd, that the interference of a churchman in political matters would not be tolerated. He continued to speak his mind, and (as the newspapers quoted him) 'to obey the commands of God before the dictates of the State'. He had close friends among African and Indian leaders, and it was said that he even got on well with certain ministers of the Dutch Reformed Church, that, in fact, *he* was behind some of the dissidents who now and then questioned Divine Sanction for the colour bar – such was the presence of his restless, black-cassocked figure, stammering eloquence, and jagged handsome face.

He had aged since she saw him last; he was less handsome. But he had still what he would have as long as he lived: the unconscious bearing of a natural prince among men that makes a celebrated actor, a political leader, a successful lover: an object of attraction and envy who, whatever his generosity of spirit, is careless of one cruelty for which other people will never forgive him – the distinction, the luck with which he was born.

He was tired and closed his eyes in a grimace straining at concentration when he talked to her, yet in spite of this, she felt the dimness of the candle of her being within his radius. Everything was right with him; nothing was quite right with her. She was only thirty-six but she had never looked any younger. Her eyes were the bright shy eyes of a young woman, but her feet and hands with their ridged nails had the look of tension and suffering of extremities that would never caress: she saw it, she saw it, she knew in his presence that they were deprived forever.

Her humiliation gave her force. She said, 'I must tell you we want him back in the tribe – I mean, there are terribly few with enough education even for administration. Within the next few years we'll desperately need more and more educated men . . . We shouldn't want him to be allowed to think of becoming a priest.'

Father Audry smiled at what he knew he was expected to come out with: that if the boy chose the way of the Lord, etc.

He said, 'What you want is someone who will turn out to be an able politician without challenging the tribal system.'

They both laughed, but, again, he had unconsciously taken the advantage of admitting their deeply divergent views; he believed the chiefs must go, while she, of course, saw no reason why Africans shouldn't develop their own tribal democracy instead of taking over the Western pattern.

'Well, he's a little young for us to be worrying about than now, don't you think?' He smiled. There were a great many papers on his desk, and she had the sense of pressure of his preoccupation with other things. 'What about the Lemeribe Mission? What's the teaching like these days – I used to know Father Chalmon when he was there—'

'I wouldn't send him to those people', she said spiritedly, implying that he knew her views on missionaries and their role in Africa. In this atmosphere of candour, they discussed Praise's background. Father Audry suggested that the boy should be encouraged to resume relations with his family, once he was back within reach of Johannesburg.

'They're pretty awful.'

'It would be best for him to acknowledge what he was, if he is to accept what he is to become.' He got up with a swish of his black skirts and strode, stooping in the opened door, to call, 'Simon, bring the boy'. Miss Graham-Grigg was smiling excitedly towards the doorway, all the will to love pacing behind the bars of her glance.

Praise entered in the navy blue shorts and white shirt of his new school uniform. The woman's kindness, the man's attention, got him in the eyes like the sun striking off the pan where the cattle had been taken to drink. Father Audry came from England, Miss Graham-Grigg had told him, like herself. That was what they were, these two white people who were not like any white people he had seen to be. What they were was being English. From far off; six thousand miles from here, as he knew from his geography book.

Praise did very well at the new school. He sang in the choir in the big church on Sundays; his body, that was to have been made a man's out in the bush, was hidden under the white robes. The boys smoked in the lavatories and once there was a girl who came and lay down for them in a storm-water ditch behind the workshops. He knew all about these things from before, on the streets and in the location where he had slept in one room with a whole family. But he did not tell the boys about the initiation. The women had not said anything to Miss Graham-Grigg. The Chief hadn't either. Soon when Praise thought about it he realized that by now it must be over. Those boys must have come back from the bush. Miss Graham-Grigg had said that after a year, when Christmas came, she would fetch him for the summer holidays. She did come and see him twice that first year, when she was down in Johannesburg, but he couldn't go back with her at Christmas because Father Audry had him in the Nativity play and was giving him personal coaching in Latin and algebra. Father Audry didn't actually teach in the school at all – it was 'his' school simply because he had begun it, and it was run by the order of which he was Father Provincial – but the reports of the boy's progress were so astonishing that, as he said to Miss Graham-Grigg, one felt one must give him all the mental stimulation one could.

'I begin to believe we may be able to sit him for his matric when he is just sixteen.' Father Audry made the pronouncement with the air of doing so at the risk of sounding ridiculous. Miss Graham-Grigg always had her hair done when she got to Johannesburg, she was looking pretty and gay. 'D'you think he could do a Cambridge entrance? My committee in London would set up a scholarship, I'm sure – investment in a future prime minister for the Protectorate!'

When Praise was sent for, she said she hardly knew him; he hadn't grown much, but he looked so *grown-up*, with his long trousers and glasses. 'You really needn't wear them when you're not working', said Father Audry. 'Well, I suppose if you take 'em on and off you keep leaving them about, eh?' They both stood back, smiling, letting the phenomenon embody in the boy.

Praise saw that she had never been reminded by anyone about the initiation. She began to give him news of his friends, Tebedi and Joseph and the others, but when he heard their names they seemed to belong to people he couldn't see in his mind.

Father Audry talked to him sometimes about what Father called his 'family', and when first he came to the school he had been told to write to them. It was a well-written, well-spelled letter in, English, exactly the letter he presented as a school exercise when one was required in class. They didn't answer. Then Father Audry must have made private efforts to get in touch with them, because the old woman, a couple of children who had been babies when he left, and one of his grown-up 'sisters' came to the school on a visiting day. They had to be pointed out to him among the other boys' visitors; he would not have known them, nor they him. He said, 'Where's my uncle?' – because he would have known him at once; he had never grown out of the slight stoop of the left shoulder where the weight of the old man's hand had impressed the young bone. But the old man was dead. Father Audry came up and put a long arm round the bent shoulder and another long arm round one of the small children and said from one to the other, 'Are you going to work hard and learn a lot like your brother?' And the small black child stared up into the nostrils filled with strong hair, the tufted eyebrows, the red mouth surrounded by the pale jowl dark-pored with beard beneath the skin, and then down, torn by fascination, to the string of beads that hung from the leather belt.

They did not come again but Praise did not much miss visitors because he spent more and more time with Father Audry. When he was not actually being coached, he was set to work to prepare his lessons or do his reading in the Father's study, where he could concentrate as one could not hope to do up at the school. Father Audry taught him chess as a form of mental gymnastics, and was jubilant the first time Praise beat him. Praise went up to the house for a game nearly every evening after supper. He tried to teach the other boys, but after the first ten minutes of explanation of moves, someone would bring out the cards or dice and they would all play one of the old games that were played in the streets and yards and locations. Johannesburg was only nine miles away; you could see the lights.

Father Audry rediscovered what Miss Graham-Grigg had found: that Praise listened attentively to music, serious music. One day Father Audry handed the boy the flute that had lain for years in its velvet-lined box that bore still the little silver name-plate: Rowland Audry. He watched while Praise gave the preliminary swaying wriggle and assumed the bent-kneed stance of all the urchin performers Father Audry had seen, and then tried to blow down it in the shy, fierce attack of penny-whistle music. Father Audry took it out of his hands. 'It's what you've just heard there.' Bach's unaccompanied flute sonata lay on the record-player. Praise smiled and frowned, giving his glasses a lift with his nose – a habit he was developing. 'But you'll soon learn to play it the right way round', said Father Audry, and with the lack of self-consciousness that comes from the habit of privilege, put the flute to his mouth and played what he remembered after ten years.

He taught Praise not only how to play the flute, but also the elements of musical composition, so that he should not simply play by ear, or simply listen with pleasure, but also understand what it was that he heard. The flute-playing was much more of a success with the boys than the chess had been, and on Saturday nights, when they sometimes made up concerts, he was allowed to take it to the hostel and play it for them. Once he played in a show for white people, in Johannesburg; but the boys could not come to that; he could only tell them about the big hall at the university, the jazz band, the African singers and dancers with their red lips and straightened hair, like white women.

The one thing that dissatisfied Father Audry was that the boy had not filled out and grown as much as one would have expected. He made it a rule that Praise must spend more time on physical exercise – the school couldn't afford a proper gymnasium, but there was some equipment outdoors. The trouble was that the boy had so little time; even with his exceptional ability, it was not going to be easy for a boy with his lack of background to matriculate at sixteen. Brother George, his form master, was certain he could be made to bring it off; there was a specially strong reason why everyone wanted him to do it since Father Audry had established that he would be eligible for an open scholarship that no black boy had ever won before – what a triumph that would be, for the boy, for the school, for all the African boys who were considered fit only for the inferior standard of 'Bantu education'! Perhaps some day this beggar child from the streets of Johannesburg might even become the first black South African to be a Rhodes Scholar. This was what Father Audry jokingly referred to as Brother George's 'sin of pride'. But who knew? It was not inconceivable. So far as the boy's physique was concerned – what Brother George said was probably true: 'You can't feed up for those years in the streets.'

From the beginning of the first term of the year he was fifteen Praise had to be coached, pressed on, and to work as even he had never worked before. His teachers gave him tremendous support; he seemed borne along on it by either arm so that he never looked up from his books. To encourage him, Father Audry arranged for him to compete in certain interschool scholastic contests that were really intended for the white Anglican schools – a spelling bee, a debate, a quiz contest. He sat on the platform in the polished halls of huge white schools and gave his correct answers in the African-accented English that the boys who surrounded him knew only as the accent of servants and delivery men.

Brother George often asked him if he were tired. But he was not tired. He only wanted to be left with his books. The boys in the hostel seemed to know this; they never asked him to play cards any more, and even when they shared smokes together in the lavatory, they passed him his drag in silence. He specially did not want Father Audry to come in with a glass of hot milk. He would rest his cheek against the pages of the books, now and then, alone in the study; that was all. The damp stone smell of the books was all he needed. Where he had once had to force himself to return again and again to the pages of things he did not grasp, gazing in blankness at the print until meaning assembled itself, he now had to force himself when it was necessary to leave the swarming facts outside which he no longer seemed to understand anything. Sometimes he could not work for minutes at a time because he was thinking that Father Audry would come in with the milk. When he did

96

come, it was never actually so bad. But Praise couldn't look at his face. Once or twice when he had gone out again, Praise shed a few tears. He found himself praying, smiling with the tears and trembling, rubbing at the scalding water that ran down inside his nose and blotched on the books.

One Saturday afternoon when Father Audry had been entertaining guests at lunch he came into the study and suggested that the boy should get some fresh air – go out and join the football game for an hour or so. But Praise was struggling with geometry problems from the previous year's matriculation paper that, to Brother George's dismay, he had suddenly got all wrong, that morning.

Father Audry could imagine what Brother George was thinking: was this an example of the phenomenon he had met with so often with African boys of a lesser calibre – the inability, through lack of an assumed cultural background, to perform a piece of work well known to them, once it was presented in a slightly different manner outside one of their own textbooks? Nonsense, of course, in this case; everyone was overanxious about the boy. Right from the start he'd shown that there was nothing mechanistic about his thought processes; he had a brain, not just a set of conditioned reflexes.

'Off you go. You'll manage better when you've taken a few knocks on the field.'

But desperation had settled on the boy's face like obstinacy. 'I must, I must', he said, putting his palms down over the books.

'Good. Then let's see if we can tackle it together.'

The black skirt swishing past the shiny shoes brought a smell of cigars. Praise kept his eyes on the black beads; the leather belt they hung from creaked as the big figure sat down. Father Audry took the chair on the opposite side of the table and switched the exercise book round towards himself. He scrubbed at the thick eyebrows till they stood out tangled, drew the hand down over his great nose, and then screwed his eyes closed a moment, mouth strangely open and lips drawn back in a familiar grimace. There was a jump, like a single painful hiccup, in Praise's body. The Father was explaining the problem gently, in his offhand English voice.

He said, 'Praise? D'you follow?' – the boy seemed sluggish,

almost deaf, as if the voice reached him as the light of a star reaches the earth from something already dead.

Father Audry put out his fine hand, in question or compassion. But the boy leapt up, dodging a blow. 'Sir – no. Sir – no.'

It was clearly hysteria; he had never addressed Father Audry as anything but 'Father'. It was some frightening retrogression, a reversion to the subconscious, a place of symbols and collective memory. He spoke for others, out of another time. Father Audry stood up but saw in alarm that by the boy's retreat he was made his pursuer, and he let him go blundering in clumsy panic out of the room.

Brother George was sent to comfort the boy. In half an hour Praise was down on the football field, running and laughing. But Father Audry took some days to get over the incident. He kept thinking how when the boy had backed away he had almost gone after him. The ugliness of the instinct repelled him; who would have thought how, at the mercy of the instinct to prey, the fox, the wild dog long for the innocence of the gentle rabbit, and the lamb. No one had shown fear of him ever before in his life. He had never given a thought to the people who were not like himself; those from whom others turn away. He felt at last a repugnant and resentful pity for them, the dripping-jawed hunters. He even thought that he would like to go into retreat for a few days, but it was inconvenient – he had so many obligations. Finally, the matter-of-factness of the boy, Praise, was the thing that restored normality. So far as the boy was concerned, one would have thought that nothing had happened. The next day he seemed to have forgotten all about it; a good thing. And so Father Audry's own inner disruption, denied by the boy's calm, sank away. He allowed the whole affair the one acknowledgment of writing to Miss Graham-Grigg – surely that was not making too much of it – to suggest that the boy was feeling the tension of his final great effort, and that a visit from her, etc.; but she was still away in England – some family troubles had kept her there for months, and in fact she had not been to see her protégé for more than a year.

Praise worked steadily on the last lap. Brother George and Father Audry watched him continuously. He was doing extremely well and seemed quite overcome with the weight of pride and pleasure when Father Audry presented him with a new black fountain pen: this was the pen with which he was to write the matriculation exam. On a Monday afternoon Father Audry, who had been in conference with the bishop all morning, looked in on his study, where every afternoon the boy would be seen sitting at the table that had been moved in for him. But there was no one there. The books were on the table. A chute of sunlight landed on the seat of the chair. Praise was not found again. The school was searched; and then the police were informed; the boys questioned; there were special prayers said in the mornings and evenings. He had not taken anything with him except the fountain pen.

When everything had been done there was nothing but silence; nobody mentioned the boy's name. But Father Audry was conducting investigations on his own. Every now and then he would get an idea that would bring a sudden hopeful relief. He wrote to Adelaide Graham-Grigg: '. . . what worries me – I believe the boy may have been on the verge of a nervous breakdown. I am hunting everywhere . . .'; was it possible that he might make his way to the Protectorate? She was acting as confidential secretary to the Chief, now, but she wrote to say that if the boy turned up she would try to make time to deal with the situation. Father Audry even sought out, at last, the 'family' – the people with whom Miss Graham-Grigg had discovered Praise living as a beggar. They had been moved to a new township and it took some time to trace them. He found Number 28b, Block E, in the appropriate ethnic group. He was accustomed to going in and out of African homes and he explained his visit to the old woman in matter-of-fact terms at once, since he knew how suspicious of questioning the people would be. There were no interior doors in these houses and a woman in the inner room who was dressing moved out of the visitor's line of vision as he sat down. She heard all that passed between Father Audry and the old woman and presently she came in with mild interest. Out of a silence the old woman was saying, 'My-my-my-my!' – she shook her head down into her bosom in a stylized expression of commiseration; they had not seen the boy. 'And he spoke so nice, everything was so nice in the school.' But they knew nothing about the boy, nothing at all. The younger woman remarked, 'Maybe he's with those boys who sleep in the old empty cars there in town – you know? – there by the beer hall?'

Something for the Time Being

He thought of it as discussing things with her, but the truth was that she did not help him out at all. She said nothing, while she ran her hand up the ridge of bone behind the rim of her child-sized yellow-brown ear, and raked her fingers tenderly into her hairline along the back of her neck as if feeling out some symptom in herself. Yet her listening was very demanding; when he stopped at the end of a supposition or a suggestion, her silence made the stop inconclusive. He had to take up again what he had said, carry it – where?

'Ve vant to give you a tsance, but you von't let us,' he mimicked; and made a loud glottal click, half angry, resentfully amused. He knew it wasn't because Kalzin Brothers were Jews that he had lost his job at last, but just because he had lost it, Mr. Solly's accent suddenly presented to him the irresistibly vulnerable. He had come out of prison nine days before after spending three months as an awaiting-trial prisoner in a political case that had just been quashed – he was one of those who would not accept bail. He had been in prison three or four times since 1952; his wife Ella and the Kalzin Brothers were used to it. Until now, his employers had always given him his job back when he came out. They were importers of china and glass and he was head packer in a team of black men who ran the dispatch department. 'Well, what the hell, I'll get something else', he said. 'Hey?'

She stopped the self-absorbed examination of the surface of her skin for a slow moment and shrugged, looking at him.

He smiled.

Her gaze loosened hold like hands falling away from a grasp. The ends of her nails pressed at small imperfections in the skin of her neck. He drank his tea and tore off pieces of bread to dip in it; then he noticed the tin of sardines she had opened, and sopped up the pale matrix of oil in which ragged flecks of silver were suspended. She offered him more tea, without speaking.

They lived in one room of a three-roomed house belonging to someone else; it was better for her that way, since he was often likely to have to be away for long stretches. She worked in a textile factory that made knitted socks; there was no one at home to look after their one child, a girl, and the child lived with a grandmother in a dusty peaceful village a day's train journey from the city.

He said, dismissing it as of no importance, 'I wonder what chance they meant? You can imagine. I don't suppose they were going to give me an office with my name on it.' He spoke as if she would appreciate the joke. She had known when she married him that he was a political man; she had been proud of him because he didn't merely want something for himself, like the other young men she knew, but everything, and for *the people*. It had excited her, under his influence, to change her awareness of herself as a young black girl to awareness of herself as belonging to the people. She knew that everything wasn't like something – a hand-out, a wangled privilege, a trinket you could hold. She would never get something from him.

Her hand went on searching over her skin as if it must come soon, come anxiously, to the flaw, the sickness, the evidence of what was wrong with her; for on this Saturday afternoon, all these things that she knew had deserted her. She had lost her wits. All that she could understand was the one room, the child growing up far away in the mud house, and the fact that you couldn't keep a job if you kept being away from work for weeks at a time.

'I think I'd better look up Flora Donaldson', he said. Flora Donaldson was a white woman who had set up an office to help political prisoners. 'Sooner the better. Perhaps she'll dig up something for me by Monday. It's the beginning of the month.'

He got on all right with those people. Ella had met Flora Donaldson once; she was a pretty white woman who looked just like any white woman who would automatically send a black face round to the back door, but she didn't seem to know that she was white and you were black.

He pulled the curtain that hung across one corner of the room and took out his suit. It was a thin suit, of the kind associated with holiday-makers in American clothing advertisements, and when he was dressed in it, with a sharp-brimmed grey hat tilted back on his small head, he looked a wiry, boyish figure, rather like one of those boy-men who sing and shake before a microphone, and whose clothes admirers try to touch as a talisman.

He kissed her good-bye, obliging her to put down, the lowering of a defence, the piece of sewing she held. She had cleared away the dishes from the table and set up the sewing machine, and he saw that the shapes of cut material that lay on the table were the parts of a small girl's dress.

She spoke suddenly. 'And when the next lot gets tired of you?'

'When that lot gets tired of me, I'll get another job again, that's all.'

She nodded, very slowly, and her hand crept back to her neck.

'Who was that?' Madge Chadders asked.

Her husband had been out into the hall to answer the telephone.

'Flora Donaldson. I wish you'd explain to these people exactly what sort of factory I've got. It's so embarrassing. She's trying to find a job for some chap, he's a skilled packer. There's no skilled packing done in my workshop, no skilled jobs at all done by black men. What on earth can I offer the fellow? She says he's desperate and anything will do.'

Madge had the broken pieces of a bowl on a newspaper spread on the Persian carpet. 'Mind the glue, darling! There, just next to your foot. Well, anything is better than nothing. I suppose it's someone who was in the Soganiland sedition case. Three months awaiting trial taken out of their lives, and now they're chucked back to fend for themselves.'

William Chadders had not had any black friends or mixed with coloured people on any but master–servant terms until he married Madge, but his views on the immorality and absurdity of the colour bar were sound; sounder, she often felt, than her own, for they were backed by the impersonal authority of a familiarity with the views of great thinkers, saints, and philosophers, with history, political economy, sociology, and anthropology. She knew only what she felt. And she always did something, at once, to express what she

102

felt. She never measured the smallness of her personal protest against the establishment she opposed; she marched with Flora and five hundred black women in a demonstration against African women being forced to carry passes; outside the university where she had once been a student, she stood between sandwich-boards bearing messages of mourning because a bill had been passed closing the university, for the future, to all but white students; she had living in her house for three months a young African who wanted to write and hadn't the peace or space to get on with it in a Location. She did not stop to consider the varying degrees of usefulness of the things she did, and if others pointed this out to her and suggested that she might make up her mind to throw her weight on the side of either politics or philanthropy, she was not resentful but answered candidly that there was so little it was possible to do that she simply took any and every chance to get off her chest her disgust at the colour bar. When she had married William Chadders, her friends had thought that her protestant activities would stop; they underestimated not only Madge, but also William, who, although he was a wealthy businessman, sub-scribed to the necessity of personal freedom as strictly as any bohemian. Besides he was not fool enough to want to change in any way the person who had enchanted him just as she was.

She reacted upon him, rather than he upon her; she, of course, would not hesitate to go ahead and change anybody. (But why not? she would have said, astonished. If it's to the good?) The attitude she sought to change would occur to her as something of independent existence, she would not see it as a cell in the organism of personality, whose whole structure would have to regroup itself round the change. She had the boldness of being unaware of these consequences.

William did not carry a banner in the streets, of course; he worked up there, among his first principles and historical prece-dents and economic necessities, but now they were translated from theory to practice of an anonymous, large-scale, and behind-the-scenes sort – he was the brains and some of the money in a scheme to get Africans some economic power besides their labour, through the setting-up of an all-African trust company and investment corporation. A number of Madge's political friends, both white and black, thought this was putting the middle-class cart before the proletarian horse, but most of the African leaders welcomed the attempt as an essential backing to popular movements on other levels – something to count on outside the unpredictability of mobs. Sometimes it amused Madge to think that William, making a point at a meeting in a boardroom, fifteen floors above life in the streets, might achieve in five minutes something of more value than she did in all her days of turning her hand to anything – from sorting old clothes to duplicating a manifesto or driving people during a bus boycott. Yet this did not knock the meaning out of her own life, for her; she knew that she had to see, touch, and talk to people in order to care about them, that was all there was to it.

Before she and her husband dressed to go out that evening, she finished sticking together the broken Chinese bowl, and showed it to him with satisfaction. To her, it was whole again. But it was one of a set, that had belonged together, and whose unity had illustrated certain philosophical concepts. William had bought them long ago, in London; for him, the whole set was damaged forever.

He said nothing to her, but he was thinking of the bowls when she said to him as they drove off, 'Will you see that chap, on Monday, yourself?'

He changed gear deliberately, attempting to follow her out of his preoccupation. But she said, 'The man Flora's sending. What was his name?'

He opened his hand on the steering wheel, indicating that the name escaped him.

'See him yourself?'

'I'll have to leave it to the works manager to find something for him to do', he said.

'Yes, I know. But see him yourself, too?'

Her anxious voice made him feel very fond of her. He turned and smiled at her suspiciously. 'Why?'

She was embarrassed at his indulgent manner. She said, frank and wheedling, 'Just to show him. You know. That you know about him and it's not much of a job.'

'All right,' he said, 'I'll see him myself.'

He met her in town straight from the office on Monday and they went to the opening of an exhibition of paintings and on to dinner and to see a play, with friends. He had not been home at all, until they returned after midnight. It was a summer night and they sat for a few minutes on their terrace, where it was still mild with the warmth of the day's sun coming from the walls in the darkness, and drank lime juice and water to quench the thirst that wine and the stuffy theatre had given them. Madge made gasps and groans of pleasure at the release from the pressures of company and noise. Then she lay quiet for a while, her voice lifting now and then in fragments of unrelated comment on the evening – the occasional chirp of a bird that has already put its head under its wing for the night.

By the time they went in, they were free of the evening. Her black dress, her earrings, and her bracelets felt like fancy dress; she shed the character and sat on the bedroom carpet, and, passing her, he said, 'Oh – that chap of Flora's came today, but I don't think he'll last. I explained to him that I didn't have the sort of job he was looking for.'

'Well, that's all right, then,' she said, inquiringly. 'What more could you do?'

'Yes,' he said, deprecating. 'But I could see he didn't like the idea much. It's a cleaner's job; nothing for him. He's an intelligent chap. I didn't like having to offer it to him.'

She was moving about her dressing table, piling out upon it the contents of her handbag. 'Then I'm sure he'll understand. It'll give him something for the time being, anyway, darling. You can't help it if you don't need the sort of work he does.'

'Huh, he won't last. I could see that. He accepted it, but only with his head. He'll get fed up. Probably won't turn up tomorrow. I had to speak to him about his Congress button, too. The works manager came to me.'

'What about his Congress button?' she said.

He was unfastening his shirt and his eyes were on the evening paper that lay folded on the bed. 'He was wearing one', he said inattentively.

'I know, but what did you have to speak to him about it for?'

'He was wearing it in the workshop all day.'

'Well, what about it?' She was sitting at her dressing table, legs spread, as if she had sat heavily and suddenly. She was not looking at him, but at her own face.

He gave the paper a push and drew his pyjamas from under

105

the pillow. Vulnerable and naked, he said authoritatively, 'You can't wear a button like that among the men in the workshop.'

'Good heavens,' she said, almost in relief, laughing, backing away from the edge of tension, chivvying him out of a piece of stuffiness. 'And why can't you?'

'You can't have someone clearly representing a political organization like Congress.'

'But he's not there *representing* anything, he's there as a workman?' Her mouth was still twitching with something between amusement and nerves.

'Exactly.'

'Then why can't he wear a button that signifies his allegiance to an organization in his private life outside the workshop? There's no rule about not wearing tie-pins or club buttons or anything, in the workshop, is there?'

'No, there isn't, but that's not quite the same thing.'

'My dear William,' she said, 'it is exactly the same. It's nothing to do with the works manager whether the man wears a Rotary button, or an Elvis Presley button, or an African National Congress button. It's damn all his business.'

'No, Madge, I'm sorry,' William said, patient, 'but it's not the same. I can give the man a job because I feel sympathetic towards the struggle he's in, but I can't put him in the workshop as a Congress man. I mean that wouldn't be fair to Fowler. That I can't do to Fowler.' He was smiling as he went towards the bathroom but his profile, as he turned into the doorway, was incisive.

She sat on at her dressing table, pulling a comb through her hair, dragging it down through knots. Then she rested her face on her palms, caught sight of herself, and became aware, against her fingers, of the curving shelf of bone, like the lip of a strong shell, under each eye. Everyone has his own intimations of mortality. For her, the feel of the bone beneath the face, in any living creature, brought her the message of the skull. Once hollowed out of this, outside the world, too. For what it's worth. It's worth a lot, the world, she affirmed, as she always did, life rising at once in her as a fish opens its jaws to a fly. It's worth a lot; and she sighed and got up with a sigh.

She went into the bathroom and sat down on the edge of the bath. He was lying there in the water, his chin relaxed on his chest, and he smiled at her. She said, 'You mean you don't want Fowler to know.'

'Oh,' he said, seeing where they were, again. 'What is it I don't want Fowler to know?'

'You don't want your partner to know that you slip black men with political ideas into your workshop. Cheeky kaffir agitators. Specially a man who's just been in jail for getting people to defy the government! – What was his name; you never said?'

'Daniel something. I don't know. Mongoma or Ngoma. Something like that.'

A line like a cut appeared between her eyebrows. 'Why can't you remember his name.' Then she went on at once, 'You don't want Fowler to know what you think, do you? That's it? You want to pretend you're like him, you don't mind the native in his place. You want to pretend that to please Fowler. You don't want Fowler to think you're cracked, or Communist, or whatever it is that good-natured, kind, jolly rich people like old Fowler think about people like us.'

'I couldn't have less interest in what Fowler thinks outside our boardroom. And inside it, he never thinks about anything but how to sell more earth-moving gear.'

'I don't mind the native in his place. You want him to think you go along with all that.' She spoke aloud, but she seemed to be telling herself rather than him.

'Fowler and I run a factory. Our only common interest is the efficient running of that factory. Our *only* one. The factory depends on a stable, satisfied black labour force, and that we've got. Right, you and I know that the whole black wage standard is too low, right, we know that they haven't a legal union to speak for them, *right*, we know that the conditions they live under make it impossible for them really to be stable. All that. But the fact is, so far as accepted standards go in this crazy country, they're a stable, satisfied labour force with better working conditions than most. So long as I'm a partner in a business that lives by them, I can't officially admit an element that represents dissatisfaction with their lot.'

'A green badge with a map of Africa on it', she said.

'If you make up your mind not to understand, you don't, and there it is', he said indulgently.

'You give him a job but you make him hide his Congress button.'

He began to soap himself. She wanted everything to stop while she inquired into things, she could not go on while a remark was unexplained or a problem unsettled, but he represented a principle she subscribed to but found so hard to follow, that life must go on, trivially, commonplace, the trailing hem of the only power worth clinging to. She smoothed the film of her thin nightgown over the shape of her knees, again and again, and presently she said, in exactly the flat tone of statement that she had used before, the flat tone that was the height of belligerence in her, 'He can say and do what he likes, he can call for strikes and boycotts and anything he likes, outside the factory, but he mustn't wear his Congress button at work.'

He was standing up, washing his body that was full of scars; she knew them all, from the place on his left breast where a piece of shrapnel had gone in, all the way back to the place under his arm where he had torn himself on barbed wire as a child. 'Yes, of course, anything he likes.'

Anything except his self-respect. Pretend, pretend. Pretend doesn't belong to a political organization. Pretend he doesn't want to be a man. Pretend he hasn't been to prison for what he believes. Suddenly she spoke to her husband. 'You'll let him have anything except the one thing worth giving.'

They stood in uncomfortable proximity to each other, in the smallness of the bathroom. They were at once aware of each other as people who live in intimacy are only when hostility returns each to the confines of himself. He felt himself naked before her, where he had stepped out on to the towelling mat, and he took a towel and slowly covered himself, pushing the free end in round his waist. She felt herself in intrusion and, in silence, went out.

Her hands were tingling. She walked up and down the bedroom floor like someone waiting to be summoned, called to account. I'll forget about it, she kept thinking, very fast, I'll forget about it again. Take a sip of water. Read another chapter. Let things flow, cover up, go on.

But when he came into the room with his wet hair combed and his stranger's face, and he said, 'You're angry', it came from her lips, a black bird in the room, before she could understand

108

what she had released – 'I'm not angry. I'm beginning to get to know you.'

Ella Mgoma knew he was going to a meeting that evening and didn't expect him home early. She put the paraffin lamp on the table so that she could see to finish the child's dress. It was done, buttons and all, by the time he came in at half past ten.

'Well, now we'll see what happens. I've got them to accept, *in principle*, that in future we won't take bail. You should have seen Ben Tsolo's face when I said that we lent the government our money interest-free when we paid bail. That really hit him. That was language he understood.' He laughed, and did not seem to want to sit down, the heat of the meeting still upon him. '*In principle*. Yes, it's easy to accept in principle. We'll see.'

She pumped the primus and set a pot of stew to warm up for him.

'Ah, that's nice' – he saw the dress. 'Finished already?' And she nodded vociferously in pleasure; but at once she noticed his forefinger run lightly along the line of braid round the neck, and the traces of failure that were always at the bottom of her cup tasted on her tongue again. Probably he was not even aware of it, or perhaps his instinct for what was true – the plumb line, the coin with the right ring – led him absently to it, but the fact was that she had botched the neck.

She had an almost Oriental delicacy about not badgering him, and she waited until he had washed and sat down to eat before she asked, 'How did the job go?'

'Oh that,' he said. 'It went.' He was eating quickly, moving his tongue strongly round his mouth to marshal the bits of meat that escaped his teeth. She was sitting with him, feeling, in spite of herself, the rest of satisfaction in her evening's work. 'Didn't you get it?'

'It got *me*. But I got loose again, all right.'

She watched his face to see what he meant. 'They don't want you to come back tomorrow?'

He shook his head, no, no, no, to stem the irritation of her suppositions. He finished his mouthful and said, 'Everything very nice. Boss takes me into his office, apologizes for the pay, he knows it's not the sort of job I should have and so forth. So I go off and clean up in the assembly shop. Then at lunch time he calls me into

109

the office again: they don't want me to wear my ANC badge at work. Flora Donaldson's sympathetic white man, who's going to do me the great favour of paying me three pounds a week.' He laughed. 'Well, there you are.'

She kept on looking at him. Her eyes widened and her mouth tightened; she was trying to prime herself to speak, or was trying not to cry. The idea of tears exasperated him and he held her with a firm, almost belligerently inquiring gaze. Her hand went up round the back of her neck under her collar, anxiously exploratory. 'Don't do that!' he said. 'You're like a monkey catching lice.'

She took her hand down swiftly and broke into trembling, like a sweat. She began to breathe hysterically. 'You couldn't put it in your pocket, for the day', she said wildly, grimacing at the bitterness of malice towards him.

He jumped up from the table. 'Christ! I knew you'd say it! I've been waiting for you to say it. You've been wanting to say it for five years. Well, now it's out. Out with it. Spit it out!' She began to scream softly as if he were hitting her. The impulse to cruelty left him and he sat down before his dirty plate, where the battered spoon lay among bits of gristle and potato eyes. Presently he spoke. 'You come out and you think there's everybody waiting for you. The truth is, there isn't anybody. You think straight in prison because you've got nothing to lose. Nobody thinks straight, outside. They don't want to hear you. What are you all going to do with me, Ella? Send me back to prison as quickly as possible? Perhaps I'll get a banishment order next time. That'd do. That's what you've got for me. I must keep myself busy with that kind of thing.'

He went over to her and said, in a kindly voice, kneading her shoulder with spread fingers, 'Don't cry. Don't cry. You're just like any other woman.'

A Chip of Glass Ruby

When the duplicating machine was brought into the house, Bamjee said, 'Isn't it enough that you've got the Indians' troubles on your back?' Mrs. Bamjee said, with a smile that showed the gap of a missing tooth but was confident all the same, 'What's the difference, Yusuf? We've all got the same troubles.'

'Don't tell me that. We don't have to carry passes; let the natives protest against passes on their own, there are millions of them. Let them go ahead with it.'

The nine Bamjee and Pahad children were present at this exchange as they were always; in the small house that held them all there was no room for privacy for the discussion of matters they were too young to hear, and so they had never been too young to hear anything. Only their sister and half-sister, Girlie, was missing; she was the eldest, and married. The children looked expectantly, unalarmed and interested, at Bamjee, who had neither left the dining-room nor settled down again to the task of rolling his own cigarettes which had been interrupted by the arrival of the duplicator. He looked at the thing that had come hidden in a wash-basket and conveyed in a black man's taxi, and the children turned on it too, their black eyes surrounded by thick lashes like those still, open flowers with hairy tentacles that close on whatever touches them.

'A fine thing to have on the dining-room table', was all he said at last. They smelled the machine among them; a smell of cold black grease. He went out, heavily on tiptoe, in his troubled way.

'It's going to go nicely on the sideboard!' Mrs. Bamjee was busy making a place by removing the two pink glass vases filled with

111

plastic carnations and the hand-painted velvet runner with the picture of the Taj Mahal.

After supper she began to run off leaflets on the machine. The family lived in the dining-room – the three other rooms in the house were full of beds – and they were all there. The older children shared a bottle of ink while they did their homework, and the two little ones pushed a couple of empty milk bottles in and out the chair legs. The three-year-old fell asleep and was carted away by one of the girls. They all drifted off to bed eventually; Bamjee himself went before the older children – he was a fruit and vegetable hawker and was up at half past four every morning to get to the market by five. 'Not long now', said Mrs. Bamjee. The older children looked up and smiled at him. He turned his back on her. She still wore the traditional clothing of a Moslem woman, and her body, which was scraggy and unimportant as a dress on a peg when it was not host to a child, was wrapped in the trailing rags of a cheap sari, and her thin black plait was greased. When she was a girl, in the Transvaal town where they lived still, her mother fixed a chip of glass ruby in her nostril; but she had abandoned that adornment as too old-style, even for her, long ago.

She was up until long after midnight, turning out leaflets. She did it as if she might have been pounding chillies.

Bamjee did not have to ask what the leaflets were. He had read the papers. All the past week Africans had been destroying their passes and then presenting themselves for arrest. Their leaders were jailed on charges of incitement, campaign offices were raided – someone must be helping the few minor leaders who were left to keep the campaign going without offices or equipment. What was it the leaflets would say – 'Don't go to work tomorrow', 'Day of Protest', 'Burn Your Pass for Freedom'? He didn't want to see.

He was used to coming home and finding his wife sitting at the dining-room table deep in discussion with strangers or people whose names were familiar by repute. Some were prominent Indians, like the lawyer, Dr. Abdul Mohammed Khan, or the big businessman, Mr. Moonsamy Patel, and he was flattered, in a suspicious way, to meet them in his house. As he came home from work next day he met Dr. Khan coming out of the house, and Dr. Khan – a highly educated man – said to him, 'A wonderful woman'. But Bamjee had never caught his wife out in any presumption; she behaved properly, as any Moslem woman should, and once her business with such gentlemen was over would never, for instance, have sat down to eat with them. He found her now back in the kitchen, setting about the preparation of dinner and carrying on a conversation on several different wave lengths with the children. 'It's really a shame if you're tired of lentils, Jimmy, because that's what you're getting – Amina, hurry up, get a pot of water going – don't worry, I'll mend that in a minute, just bring the yellow cotton, and there's a needle in the cigarette box on the sideboard.'

'Was that Dr. Khan leaving?' said Bamjee.

'Yes, there's going to be a stay-at-home on Monday. Desai's ill, and he's got to get the word around by himself. Bob Jali was up all last night printing leaflets, but he's gone to have a tooth out.' She had always treated Bamjee as if it were only a mannerism that made him appear uninterested in politics, the way some woman will persist in interpreting her husband's bad temper as an endearing gruffness hiding boundless goodwill, and she talked to him of these things just as she passed on to him neighbours' or family gossip.

'What for do you want to get mixed up with these killings and stonings and I don't know what? Congress should keep out of it. Isn't it enough with the Group Areas?'

She laughed. 'Now, Yusuf, you know you don't believe that. Look how you said the same thing when the Group Areas started in Natal. You said we should begin to worry when we get moved out of our own houses here in the Transvaal. And then your own mother lost her house in Noorddorp, and there you are; you saw that nobody's safe. Oh, Girlie was here this afternoon, she says Ismail's brother's engaged – that's nice, isn't it? His mother will be pleased; she was worried.'

'Why was she worried?' asked Jimmy, who was fifteen, and old enough to patronize his mother.

'Well, she wanted to see him settled. There's a party on Sunday week at Ismail's place – you'd better give me your suit to give to the cleaners tomorrow, Yusuf.'

One of the girls presented herself at once. 'I'll have nothing to wear, Ma.'

Mrs. Bamjee scratched her sallow face. 'Perhaps Girlie will lend you her pink, eh? Run over to Girlie's place now and say I say will she lend it to you.'

The sound of commonplaces often does service as security, and Bamjee, going to sit in the armchair with the shiny armrests that was wedged between the dining-room table and the sideboard, lapsed into an unthinking doze that, like all times of dreamlike ordinariness during those weeks, was filled with uneasy jerks and starts back into reality. The next morning, as soon as he got to market, he heard that Dr. Khan had been arrested. But that night Mrs. Bamjee sat up making a new dress for her daughter; the sight disarmed Bamjee, reassured him again, against his will, so that the resentment he had been making ready all day faded into a morose and accusing silence. Heaven knew, of course, who came and went in the house during the day. Twice in that week of riots, raids, and arrests, he found black women in the house when he came home; plain ordinary native women in doeks, drinking tea. This was not a thing other Indian women would have in their homes, he thought bitterly; but then his wife was not like other people, in a way he could not put his finger on, except to say what it was not: not scandalous, not punishable, not rebellious. It was, like the attraction that had led him to marry her, Pahad's widow with five children, something he could not see clearly.

When the Special Branch knocked steadily on the door in the small hours of Thursday morning, he did not wake up, for his return to consciousness was always set in his mind to half past four, and that was more than an hour away. Mrs. Bamjee got up herself, struggled into Jimmy's raincoat, which was hanging over a chair, and went to the front door. The clock on the wall – a wedding present when she married Pahad – showed three o'clock when she snapped on the light, and she knew at once who it was on the other side of the door. Although she was not surprised, her hands shook like a very old person's as she undid the locks and the complicated catch on the wire burglar-proofing. And then she opened the door and they were there – two coloured policemen in plain clothes. 'Zanip Bamjee?'

'Yes'.

As they talked, Bamjee woke up in the sudden terror of having overslept. Then he became conscious of men's voices. He heaved himself out of bed in the dark and went to the window, which, like the front door, was covered with a heavy mesh of thick wire against intruders from the dingy lane it looked upon. Bewildered, he appeared in the dining-room, where the policemen were searching through a soapbox of papers beside the duplicating machine. 'Yusuf, it's for me', Mrs. Bamjee said.

At once, the snap of a trap, realization came. He stood there in an old shirt before the two policemen, and the woman was going off to prison because of the natives. 'There you are!' he shouted, standing away from her. 'That's what you've got for it. Didn't I tell you? Didn't I? That's the end of it now. That's the finish. That's what it's come to.' She listened with her head at the slightest tilt to one side, as if to ward off a blow, or in compassion.

Jimmy, Pahad's son, appeared at the door with a suitcase; two or three of the girls were behind him. 'Here, Ma, you take my green jersey.' 'I've found your clean blouse.' Bamjee had to keep moving out of their way as they helped their mother to make ready. It was like the preparation for one of the family festivals his wife made such a fuss over; wherever he put himself, they bumped into him. Even the two policemen mumbled, 'Excuse me', and pushed past into the rest of the house to continue their search. They took with them a tome that Nehru had written in prison; it had been bought from a persevering travelling salesman and kept, for years, on the mantelpiece. 'Oh, don't take that, please,' Mrs. Bamjee said suddenly, clinging to the arm of the man who had picked it up.

The man held it away from her.

'What does it matter, Ma?'

It was true that no one in the house had ever read it; but she said, 'It's for my children.'

'Ma, leave it.' Jimmy, who was squat and plump, looked like a merchant advising a client against a roll of silk she had set her heart on. She went into the bedroom and got dressed. When she came out in her old yellow sari with a brown coat over it, the faces of the children were behind her like faces on the platform at a railway station. They kissed her good-bye. The policemen did not hurry her, but she seemed to be in a hurry just the same.

'What am I going to do?' Bamjee accused them all.

The policemen looked away patiently.

'It'll be all right. Girlie will help. The big children can manage. And Yusuf—' The children crowded in around her; two of the younger ones had awakened and appeared, asking shrill questions.

'Come on', said the policemen.

'I want to speak to my husband.' She broke away and came back to him, and the movement of her sari hid them from the rest of the room for a moment. His face hardened in suspicious anticipation against the request to give some message to the next fool who would take up her pamphleteering until he, too, was arrested. 'On Sunday,' she said. 'Take them on Sunday.' He did not know what she was talking about. 'The engagement party,' she whispered, low and urgent. 'They shouldn't miss it. Ismail will be offended.'

They listened to the car drive away. Jimmy bolted and barred the front door, and then at once opened it again; he put on the raincoat that his mother had taken off. 'Going to tell Girlie', he said. The children went back to bed. Their father did not say a word to any of them; their talk, the crying of the younger ones and the argumentative voices of the older, went on in the bedrooms. He found himself alone; he felt the night all around him. And then he happened to meet the clock face and saw with a terrible sense of unfamiliarity that this was not the secret night but an hour he should have recognized: the time he always got up. He pulled on his trousers and his dirty white hawker's coat and wound his grey muffler up to the stubble on his chin and went to work.

The duplicating machine was gone from the sideboard. The policemen had taken it with them, along with the pamphlets and the conference reports and the stack of old newspapers that had collected on top of the wardrobe in the bedroom – not the thick dailies of the white men, but the thin, impermanent-looking papers that spoke up, sometimes interrupted by suppression or lack of money, for the rest. It was all gone. When he had married her and moved in with her and her five children, into what had been the Pahad and became the Bamjee house, he had not recognized the humble, harmless, and apparently useless routine tasks – the minutes of meetings being written up on the dining-room table at night, the government blue books that were read while the latest baby was suckled, the employment of the fingers of the older children in the fashioning of crinkle-paper Congress rosettes – as activity intended to move mountains. For years and years he had not noticed it, and now it was gone.

The house was quiet. The children kept to their lairs, crowded on the beds with the doors shut. He sat and looked at the sideboard, where the plastic carnations and the mat with the picture of the Taj Mahal were in place. For the first few weeks he never spoke of her. There was the feeling, in the house, that he had wept and raged at her, that boulders of reproach had thundered down upon her absence, and yet he had said not one word. He had not been to inquire where she was; Jimmy and Girlie had gone to Mohammed Ebrahim, the lawyer, and when he found out that their mother had been taken – when she was arrested, at least – to a prison in the next town, they had stood about outside the big prison door for hours while they waited to be told where she had been moved from there. At last they had discovered that she was fifty miles away, in Pretoria. Jimmy asked Bamjee for five shillings to help Girlie pay the train fare to Pretoria, once she had been interviewed by the police and had been given a permit to visit her mother; he put three two-shilling pieces on the table for Jimmy to pick up, and the boy, looking at him keenly, did not know whether the extra shilling meant anything, or whether it was merely that Bamjee had no change.

It was only when relations and neighbours came to the house that Bamjee would suddenly begin to talk. He had never been so expansive in his life as he was in the company of these visitors, many of them come on a polite call rather in the nature of a visit of condolence. 'Ah, yes, yes, you can see how I am – you see what has been done to me. Nine children, and I am on the cart all day. I get home at seven or eight. What are you to do? What can people like us do?'

'Poor Mrs. Bamjee. Such a kind lady.'

'Well, you see for yourself. They walk in here in the middle of the night and leave a houseful of children. I'm out on the cart all day, I've got a living to earn.' Standing about in his shirt sleeves, he became quite animated; he would call for the girls to bring fruit drinks for the visitors. When they were gone, it was as if he, who was orthodox if not devout and never drank liquor, had been

117

drunk and abruptly sobered up; he looked dazed and could not have gone over in his mind what he had been saying. And as he cooled, the lump of resentment and wrongedness stopped his throat again.

Bamjee found one of the little boys the centre of a self-important group of championing brothers and sisters in the dining-room one evening. 'They've been cruel to Ahmed.'

'What has he done?' said the father.

'Nothing! Nothing!' The little girl stood twisting her hand-kerchief excitedly.

An older one, thin as her mother, took over, silencing the others with a gesture of her skinny hand. 'They did it at school today. They made an example of him.'

'What is an example?' said Bamjee impatiently.

'The teacher made him come up and stand in front of the whole class, and he told them, "You see this boy? His mother's in jail because she likes the natives so much. She wants the Indians to be the same as natives."'

'It's terrible,' he said. His hands fell to his sides. 'Did she ever think of this?'

'That's why Ma's *there*,' said Jimmy, putting aside his comic and emptying out his schoolbooks upon the table. 'That's all the kids need to know. Ma's there because things like this happen. Petersen's a coloured teacher, and it's his black blood that's brought him trouble all his life, I suppose. He hates anyone who says every-body's the same, because that takes away from 'im his bit of whiteness that's all he's got. What d'you expect? it's nothing to make too much fuss about.'

'Of course, you are fifteen and you know everything,' Bamjee mumbled at him.

'I don't say that. But I know Ma, anyway.' The boy laughed.

There was a hunger strike among the political prisoners, and Bamjee could not bring himself to ask Girlie if her mother was starving herself too. He would not ask; and yet he saw in the young woman's face the gradual weakening of her mother. When the strike had gone on for nearly a week one of the elder children burst into tears at the table and could not eat. Bamjee pushed his own plate away in rage.

Sometimes he spoke out loud to himself while he was driving the vegetable lorry. 'What for?' Again and again: 'What for?' She was not a modern woman who cut her hair and wore short skirts. He had married a good plain Moslem woman who bore children and stamped her own chillies. He had a sudden vision of her at the duplicating machine, that night just before she was taken away, and he felt himself maddened, baffled, and hopeless. He had become the ghost of a victim, hanging about the scene of a crime whose motive he could not understand and had not had time to learn.

The hunger strike at the prison went into the second week. Alone in the rattling cab of his lorry, he said things that he heard as if spoken by someone else, and his heart burned in fierce agreement with them. 'For a crowd of natives who'll smash our shops and kill us in our houses when their time comes.' 'She will starve herself to death there.' 'She will die there.' 'Devils who will burn and kill us.' He fell into bed each night like a stone, and dragged himself up in the mornings as a beast of burden is beaten to its feet.

One of these mornings, Girlie appeared very early, while he was wolfing bread and strong tea – alternate sensations of dry solidity and stinging heat – at the kitchen table. Her real name was Fatima, of course, but she had adopted the silly modern name along with the clothes of the young factory girls among whom she worked. She was expecting her first baby in a week or two, and her small face, her cut and curled hair, and the sooty arches drawn over her eyebrows did not seem to belong to her thrust-out body under a clean smock. She wore mauve lipstick and was smiling her cocky little white girl's smile, foolish and bold, not like an Indian girl's at all.

'What's the matter?' he said.

She smiled again. 'Don't you know? I told Bobby he must get me up in time this morning. I wanted to be sure I wouldn't miss you today.'

'I don't know what you're talking about.'

She came over and put her arm up around his unwilling neck and kissed the grey bristles at the side of his mouth. 'Many happy returns! Don't you know it's your birthday?'

'No,' he said. 'I didn't know, didn't think—' He broke the pause by swiftly picking up the bread and giving his attention desperately to eating and drinking. His mouth was busy, but his eyes looked at her, intensely black. She said nothing, but stood there with him. She would not speak, and at last he said, swallowing a piece of bread that tore at his throat as it went down, 'I don't remember these things.'

The girl nodded, the Woolworth baubles in her ears swinging. 'That's the first thing she told me when I saw her yesterday – don't forget it's Bajie's birthday tomorrow.'

He shrugged over it. 'It means a lot to children. But that's how she is. Whether it's one of the old cousins or the neighbour's grandmother, she always knows when the birthday is. What importance is my birthday, while she's sitting there in a prison? I don't understand how she can do the things she does when her mind is always full of woman's nonsense at the same time – that's what I don't understand with her.'

'Oh, but don't you see?' the girl said. 'It's because she doesn't want anybody to be left out. It's because she always remembers; remembers everything – people without somewhere to live, hungry kids, boys who can't get educated – remembers all the time. That's how Ma is.'

'Nobody else is like that.' It was half a complaint.

'No, nobody else', said his stepdaughter.

She sat herself down at the table, resting her belly. He put his head in his hands. 'I'm getting old' – but he was overcome by something much more curious, by an answer. He knew why he had desired her, the ugly widow with five children; he knew what way it was in which she was not like the others; it was there, like the fact of the belly that lay between him and her daughter.

Some Monday for Sure

My sister's husband, Josias, used to work on the railways but then he got this job where they make dynamite for the mines. He was the one who sits out on that little iron seat clamped to the back of the big red truck, with a red flag in his hand. The idea is that if you drive up too near the truck or look as if you're going to crash into it, he waves the flag to warn you off. You've seen those trucks often on the Main Reef Road between Johannesburg and the mining towns – they carry the stuff and have DANGER – EXPLOSIVES painted on them. The man sits there, with an iron chain looped across his little seat to keep him from being thrown into the road, and he clutches his flag like a kid with a balloon. That's how Josias was, too. Of course, if you didn't take any notice of the warning and went on and crashed into the truck, he would be the first to be blown to high heaven and hell, but he always just sits there, this chap, as if he has no idea when he was born or that he might not die on a bed an old man of eighty. As if the dust in his eyes and the racket of the truck are going to last forever.

My sister knew she had a good man but she never said anything about being afraid of this job. She only grumbled in winter, when he was stuck out there in the cold and used to get a cough (she's a nurse), and on those times in summer when it rained all day and she said he would land up with rheumatism, crippled, and then who would give him work? The dynamite people? I don't think it ever came into her head that any day, every day, he could be blown up instead of coming home in the evening. Anyway, you wouldn't have thought so by the way she took it when he told us what it was he was going to have to do.

I was working down at a garage in town, that time, at the petrol

121

pumps, and I was eating before he came in because I was on night shift. Emma had the water ready for him and he had a wash without saying much, as usual, but then he didn't speak when they sat down to eat, either, and when his fingers went into the mealie meal he seemed to forget what it was he was holding and not to be able to shape it into a mouthful. Emma must have thought he felt too dry to eat, because she got up and brought him a jam tin of the beer she had made for Saturday. He drank it and then sat back and looked from her to me, but she said, 'Why don't you eat?' and he began to, slowly. She said, 'What's the matter with you?' He got up and yawned and yawned, showing those brown chipped teeth that remind me of the big ape at the Johannesburg zoo that I saw once when I went with the school. He went into the other room of the house, where he and Emma slept, and he came back with his pipe. He filled it carefully, the way a poor man does; I saw, as soon as I went to work at the filling station, how the white men fill their pipes, stuffing the tobacco in, picking out any bits they don't like the look of, shoving the tin half shut back into the glove box of the car. 'I'm going down to Sela's place,' said Emma. 'I can go with Willie on his way to work if you don't want to come.'

'No. Not tonight. You stay here.' Josias always speaks like this, the short words of a schoolmaster or a boss-boy, but if you hear the way he says them, you know he is not really ordering you around at all, he is only asking you.

'No, I told her I'm coming', Emma said, in the voice of a woman having her own way in a little thing.

'Tomorrow.' Josias began to yawn again, looking at us with wet eyes. 'Go to bed,' Emma said. 'I won't be late.'

'No, no, I want to . . .' He blew a sigh. 'When he's gone, man—' He moved his pipe at me. 'I'll tell you later.'

Emma laughed. 'What can you tell that Willie can't hear.' I've lived with them ever since they were married. Emma always was the one who looked after me, even before, when I was a little kid. It was true that whatever happened to us happened to us together. He looked at me; I suppose he saw that I was a man, now: I was in my blue overalls with *Shell* on the pocket and everything.

He said, 'They want me to do something . . . a job with the truck.'

Josias used to turn out regularly to political meetings and he took part in a few protests before everything went underground, but he had never been more than one of the crowd. We had Mandela and the rest of the leaders, cut out of the paper, hanging on the wall, but he had never known, personally, any of them. Of course there were his friends Ndhlovu and Seb Masinde who said they had gone underground and who occasionally came late at night for a meal or slept in my bed for a few hours.

'They want to stop the truck on the road—'

'Stop it?' Emma was like somebody stepping into cold dark water; with every word that was said she went deeper. 'But how can you do it – when? Where will they do it?' She was wild, as if she must go out and prevent it all happening right then.

I felt that cold water of Emma's rising round the belly because Emma and I often had the same feelings, but I caught also, in Josias's not looking at me, a signal Emma couldn't know. Something in me jumped at it like catching a swinging rope. 'They want the stuff inside . . .?'

Nobody said anything.

I said, 'What a lot of big bangs you could make with that, man', and then shut up before Josias needed to tell me to.

'So what're you going to do?' Emma's mouth stayed open after she had spoken, the lips pulled back.

'They'll tell me everything. I just have to give them the best place on the road – that'll be the Free State road, the others're too busy . . . and . . . the time when we pass . . .'

'You'll be dead.' Emma's head was shuddering and her whole body shook; I've never seen anybody give up like that. He was dead already, she saw it with her eyes and she was kicking and screaming without knowing how to show it to him. She looked like she wanted to kill Josias herself, for being dead. 'That'll be the finish, for sure. He's got a gun, the white man in front, hasn't he, you told me. And the one with him? They'll kill you. You'll go to prison. They'll take you to Pretoria jail and hang you by the rope . . . Yes, he's got the gun, you told me, didn't you – many times you told me—'

'The others've got guns too. How d'you think they can hold us up? They've got guns and they'll come all round him. It's all worked out—'

'The one in front will shoot you, I know it, don't tell me, I know what I say . . .' Emma went up and down and around till I

123

thought she would push the walls down – they wouldn't have needed much pushing, in that house in Tembekile Location – and I was scared of her. I don't mean for what she would do to me if I got in her way, or to Josias, but for what might happen to her: something like taking a fit or screaming that none of us would be able to forget.

I don't think Josias was sure about doing the job before but he wanted to do it now. 'No shooting. Nobody will shoot me. Nobody will know that I know anything. Nobody will know I tell them anything. I'm held up just the same like the others! Same as the white man in front! Who can shoot me? They can shoot me for that?'

'Someone else can go, I don't want it, do you hear? You will stay at home, I will say you are sick . . . You will be killed, they will shoot you . . . Josias, I'm telling you, I don't want . . . I won't . . .'

I was waiting my chance to speak, all the time, and I felt Josias was waiting to talk to someone who had caught the signal. I said quickly, while she went on and on, 'But even on that road there are some cars?'

'Roadblocks,' he said, looking at the floor. 'They've got the signs, the ones you see when a road's being dug up, and there'll be some men with picks. After the truck goes through they'll block the road so that any other cars turn off on to the old road there by Kalmansdrif. The same thing on the other side, two miles on. There where the farm road goes down to Nek Halt.'

'Hell, man! Did you have to pick what part of the road?'

'I know it like this yard. Don't I?'

Emma stood there, between the two of us, while we discussed the whole business. We didn't have to worry about anyone hearing, not only because Emma kept the window wired up in that kitchen, but also because the yard the house was in was a real Tembekile Location one, full of babies yelling and people shouting, night and day, not to mention the transistors playing in the houses all round. Emma was looking at us all the time and out of the corner of my eye I could see her big front going up and down fast in the neck of her dress.

'. . . so they're going to tie you up as well as the others?'

He drew on his pipe to answer me.

We thought for a moment and then grinned at each other; it was the first time for Josias, that whole evening.

Emma began collecting the dishes under our noses. She dragged the tin bath of hot water from the stove and washed up. 'I said I'm taking my off on Wednesday. I suppose this is going to be next week.' Suddenly, yet talking as if carrying on where she let up, she was quite different.

'I don't know.'

'Well, I have to know because I suppose I must be at home.'

'What must you be at home for?' said Josias.

'If the police come I don't want them talking to *him*', she said, looking at us both without wanting to see us.

'The police—' said Josias, and jerked his head to send them running, while I laughed, to show her.

'And I want to know what I must say.'

'What must you say? Why? They can get my statement from me when they find us tied up. In the night I'll be back here myself.'

'Oh yes', she said, scraping the mealie meal he hadn't eaten back into the pot. She did everything as usual; she wanted to show us nothing was going to wait because of this big thing, she must wash the dishes and put ash on the fire. 'You'll be back, oh yes. – Are you going to sit here all night. Willie? – Oh yes, you'll be back.'

And then, I think, for a moment Josias saw himself dead, too; he didn't answer when I took my cap and said, so long, from the door.

I knew it must be a Monday. I notice that women quite often don't remember ordinary things like this, I don't know what they think about – for instance, Emma didn't catch on that it must be Monday, next Monday or the one after, some Monday for sure, because Monday was the day that we knew Josias went with the truck to the Free State mines. It was Friday when he told us and all day Saturday I had a terrible feeling that it was going to be *that* Monday, and it would be all over before I could – what? I didn't know, man. I felt I must at least see where it was going to happen. Sunday I was off work and I took my bicycle and rode into town before there was even anybody in the streets and went to the big station and found that although there wasn't a train on Sundays that would take me all the way, I could get one that would take me about thirty miles. I had to pay to put the bike in the luggage van as well as for my ticket, but I'd got my wages on Friday. I got off at the nearest halt to Kalmansdrif and then I asked people along the road the best way. It was a long ride, more than two hours. I came out on the main road from the sand road just at the turn-off Josias had told me about. It was just like he said: a tin sign KALMANSDRIF pointing down the road I'd come from. And the nice blue tarred road, smooth, straight ahead: was I glad to get on to it! I hadn't taken much notice of the country so far, while I was sweating along, but from then on I woke up and saw everything. I've only got to think about it to see it again now. The veld is flat round about there, it was the end of winter, so the grass was dry. Quite far away and very far apart, there was a hill, and then another, sticking up in the middle of nothing, pink colour, and with its point cut off like the neck of a bottle. Ride and ride, these hills never got any nearer and there were none beside the road. It all looked empty and the sky much bigger than the ground, but there were some people there. It's funny you don't notice them like you do in town. All our people, of course; there were barbed-wire fences, so it must have been white farmers' land, but they've got the water and their houses are far off the road and you can usually see them only by the big dark trees that hide them. Our people had mud houses and there would be three or four in the same place made bare by goats and people's feet. Often the huts were near a kind of crack in the ground, where the little kids played and where, I suppose, in summer, there was water. Even now the women were managing to do washing in some places. I saw children run to the road to jig about and stamp when cars passed, but the men and women took no interest in what was up there. It was funny to think that I was just like them, now, men and women who are always busy inside themselves with jobs, plans, thinking about how to get money or how to talk to someone about something important, instead of like the children, as I used to be only a few years ago, taking in each small thing around them as it happens.

Still, there were people living pretty near the road. What would they do if they saw the dynamite truck held up and a fight going on? (I couldn't think of it, then, in any other way except like I'd seen hold-ups in Westerns, although I've seen plenty of fighting, all my life, among the Location gangs and drunks – I was ashamed not to be able to forget those kid-stuff Westerns at a time like this.) Would

126

they go running away to the white farmer? Would somebody jump on a bike and go for the police? Or if there was no bike, what about a horse? I saw someone riding a horse.

I rode slowly to the next turn-off, the one where a farm road goes down to Nek Halt. There it was, just like Josias said. Here was where the other roadblock would be. But when he spoke about it there was nothing in between! No people, no houses, no flat veld with hills on it! It had been just one of those things grown-ups see worked out in their heads: while all the time, here it was, a real place where people had cooking fires, I could hear a herdboy yelling at a dirty bundle of sheep, a big bird I've never seen in town balanced on the barbed-wire fence right in front of me . . . I got off my bike and it flew away.

I sat a minute on the side of the road. I'd had a cold drink in an Indian shop in the dorp where I'd got off the train, but I was dry again inside my mouth, while plenty of water came out of my skin, I can tell you. I rode back down the road looking for the exact place I would choose if I were Josias. There was a stretch where there was only one kraal consisting of two houses, and that quite a way back from the road. Also there was a dip where the road went over a donga. Old stumps of trees and nothing but cows' business down there; men could hide. I got off again and had a good look round.

But I wondered about the people, up top. I don't know why it was, I wanted to know about those people just as though I was going to have to go and live with them, or something. I left the bike down in the donga and crossed the road behind a Cadillac going so fast the air smacked together after it, and I began to trek over the veld to the houses. I know most of our people live like this, in the veld, but I'd never been into houses like that before. I was born in some Location (I don't know which one, I must ask Emma one day) and Emma and I lived in Goughville Location with our grandmother. Our mother worked in town and she used to come and see us sometimes, but we never saw our father and Emma thinks that perhaps we didn't have the same father, because she remembers a man before I was born, and after I was born she didn't see him again. I don't really remember anyone, from when I was a little kid, except Emma. Emma dragging me along so fast my arm almost came off my body, because we had nearly been

127

caught by the Indian while stealing peaches from his lorry: we did that every day.

We lived in one room with our grandmother but it was a tin house with a number and later on there was a streetlight at the corner. These houses I was coming to had a pattern all over them marked into the mud they were built of. There was a mound of dried cows' business, as tall as I was, stacked up in a pattern, too. And then the usual junk our people have, just like in the Location: old tins, broken things collected in white people's rubbish heaps. The fowls ran sideways from my feet and two old men let their talking die away into ahas and ehês as I came up. I greeted them the right way to greet old men and they nodded and went on ehêing and ahaing to show that they had been greeted properly. One of them had very clean ragged trousers tied with string and sat on the ground, but the other, sitting on a bucket seat that must have been taken from some scrapyard car, was dressed in a way I've never seen – from the old days, I suppose. He wore a black suit with very wide trousers, laced boots, a stiff white collar and black tie, and on top of it all, a broken old hat. It was Sunday, of course, so I suppose he was all dressed up. I've heard that these people who work for farmers wear sacks most of the time. The old ones didn't ask me what I wanted there. They just peered at me with their eyes gone the colour of soapy water because they were so old. And I didn't know what to say because I hadn't thought what I was going to say, I'd just walked. Then a little kid slipped out of the dark doorway quick as a cockroach. I thought perhaps everyone else was out because it was Sunday but then a voice called from inside the other house, and when the child didn't answer, called again, and a woman came to the doorway.

I said my bicycle had a puncture and could I have some water.

She said something into the house and in a minute a girl, about fifteen she must've been, edged past her carrying a paraffin tin and went off to fetch water. Like all the girls that age, she never looked at you. Her body shook under an ugly old dress and she almost hobbled in her hurry to get away. Her head was tied up in a rag-doek right down to the eyes the way old-fashioned people do, otherwise she would have been quite pretty, like any other girl. When she had gone a little way the kid went pumping after her, panting, yelling, opening his skinny legs wide as scissors over stones and antheaps, and then he caught up with her and you could see that right away she was quite different, I knew how it was, she yelled at him, you heard her laughter as she dashed him with the tin, whirled around from out of his clutching hands, struggled with him; they were together like Emma and I used to be when we got away from the old lady, and from the school, and everybody. And Emma was also one of our girls who have the big strong comfortable bodies of mothers even when they're still kids, maybe it comes from always lugging the smaller one round on their backs.

A man came out of the house behind the woman and was friendly. His hair had the dusty look of someone who's been sleeping off drink. In fact, he was still a bit heavy with it.

'You coming from Jo'burg?'

But I wasn't going to be caught out being careless at all, Josias could count on me for that.

'Vereeniging.'

He thought there was something funny there – nobody dresses like a Jo'burger, you could always spot us a mile off – but he was too full to follow it up.

He stood stretching his sticky eyelids open and then he fastened on me the way some people will do: 'Can't you get me work there where you are?'

'What kind of work?'

He waved a hand describing me. 'You got a good work.'

''Sall right.'

'Where you working now?'

'Garden boy.'

He tittered, 'Look like you work in town', shook his head.

I was surprised to find the woman handing me a tin of beer, and I squatted on the ground to drink it. It's mad to say that a mud house can be pretty, but those patterns made in the mud looked nice. They must have been done with a sharp stone or stick when the mud was smooth and wet, the shapes of things like big leaves and moons filled in with lines that went all one way in this shape, another way in that, so that as you looked at the walls in the sun, some shapes were dark and some were light, and if you moved, the light ones went dark and the dark ones got light instead. The girl came back with the heavy tin of water on her head making her

129

neck thick. I washed out the jam tin I'd had the beer in and filled it with water. When I thanked them, the old men stirred and ahaed and eheed again. The man made as if to walk a bit with me, but I was lucky, he didn't go more than a few yards. 'No good,' he said. 'Every morning, five o'clock, and the pay – very small.'

How I would have hated to be him, a man already married and with big children, working all his life in the fields wearing sacks. When you think like this about someone he seems something you could never possibly be, as if it's his fault, and not just the chance of where he happened to be born. At the same time I had a crazy feeling I wanted to tell him something wonderful, something he'd never dreamed could happen, something he'd fall on his knees and thank me for. I wanted to say, 'Soon you'll be the farmer yourself and you'll have shoes like me and your girl will get water from your windmill. Because on Monday, or another Monday, the truck will stop down there and all the stuff will be taken away and they – Josias, me; even you, yes – we'll win forever.' But instead all I said was, 'Who did that on your house?' He didn't understand and I made a drawing in the air with my hand. 'The women', he said, not interested.

Down in the donga I sat a while and then threw away the tin and rode off without looking up again to where the kraal was.

It wasn't that Monday. Emma and Josias go to bed very early and of course they were asleep by the time I got home late on Sunday night – Emma thought I'd been with the boys I used to go around with at weekends. But Josias got up at half past four every morning, then, because it was a long way from the Location to where the dynamite factory was, and although I didn't usually even hear him making the fire in the kitchen which was also where I was sleeping, that morning I was awake the moment he got out of bed next door. When he came into the kitchen I was sitting up in my blankets and I whispered loudly, 'I went there yesterday. I saw the turn-off and everything. Down there by the donga, ay? Is that the place?'

He looked at me, a bit dazed. He nodded. Then: 'Wha'd you mean you went there?'

'I could see that's the only good place. I went up to the houses, too, just to see . . . the people are all right. Not many. When it's not

130

Sunday there may be nobody there but the old man – there were two, I think one was just a visitor. The man and the women will be over in the fields somewhere, and that must be quite far, because you can't see the mealies from the road . . .' I could feel myself being listened to carefully, getting in with him (and if with him, with *them*) while I was talking, and I knew exactly what I was saying, absolutely clearly, just as I would know exactly what I was doing. He began to question me; but like I was an older man or a clever one; he didn't know what to say. He drank his tea while I told him all about it. He was thinking. Just before he left he said, 'I shouldn't't've told you.'

I ran after him, outside, into the yard. It was still dark. I blurted in the same whisper we'd been using, 'Not today, is it?' I couldn't see his face properly but I knew he didn't know whether to answer or not. 'Not today'. I was so happy I couldn't go to sleep again.

In the evening Josias managed to make some excuse to come out with me alone for a bit. He said, 'I told them you were a hundred-per-cent. It's just the same as if I know.' 'Of course, no difference. I just haven't had much of a chance to do anything . . .' I didn't carry on: '. . . because I was too young'; we didn't want to bring Emma into it. And anyway, no one but a real kid is too young any more. Look at the boys who are up for sabotage. I said, 'Have they got them all?'

He hunched his shoulders.

'I mean, even the ones for the picks and spades . . . ?'

He wouldn't say anything, but I knew I could ask. 'Oh, boetie, man, even just to keep a lookout, there on the road . . .'

I know he didn't want it but once they knew I knew, and that I'd been there and everything, they were keen to use me. At least that's what I think. I never went to any meetings or anything where it was planned, and beforehand I only met the two others who were with me at the turn-off in the end, and we were told exactly what we had to do by Seb Masinde. Of course, neither of us said a word to Emma. The Monday that we did it was three weeks later and I can tell you, although a lot's happened to me since then, I'll never forget the moment when we flagged the truck through with Josias sitting there on the back in his little seat. Josias!

I wanted to laugh and shout there in the veld; I didn't feel scared – what was there to be scared of, he'd been sitting on a load of dynamite every day of his life for years now, so what's the odds. We had one of those tins of fire and a bucket of tar and the real ROAD CLOSED signs from the PWD and everything went smooth at our end. It was at the Nek Halt end that the trouble started when one of these AA patrol bikes had to come along (Josias says it was something new, they'd never met a patrol on that road that time of day, before) and get suspicious about the block there. In the meantime the truck was stopped all right but someone was shot and Josias tried to get the gun from the white man up in front of the truck and there was a hell of a fight and they had to make a getaway with the stuff in a car and van back through our block, instead of taking over the truck and driving it to a hiding place to offload. More than half the stuff had to be left behind in the truck. Still, they got clean away with what they did get and it was never found by the police. Whenever I read in the papers here that something's been blown up back at home, I wonder if it's still one of our bangs. Two of our people got picked up right away and some more later and the whole thing was all over the papers with speeches by the chief of Special Branch about a master plot and everything. But Josias got away okay. We three chaps at the road-block just ran into the veld to where there were bikes hidden. We went to a place we'd been told in Rustenburg district for a week and then we were told to get over to Bechuanaland. It wasn't so bad; we had no money but around Rustenburg it was easy to pinch paw-paws and oranges off the farms . . . Oh, I sent a message to Emma that I was all right; and at that time it didn't seem true that I couldn't go home again.

But in Bechuanaland it was different. We had no money, and you don't find food on trees in that dry place. They said they would send us money; it didn't come. But Josias was there too, and we stuck together; people hid us and we kept going. Planes arrived and took away the big shots and the white refugees but although we were told we'd go too, it never came off. We had no money to pay for ourselves. There were plenty others like us in the beginning. At last we just walked, right up Bechuanaland and through Northern Rhodesia to Mbeya, that's over the border in Tanganyika, where we were headed for. A long walk; took Josias and me months. We met up with a chap who'd been given a bit of money and from there sometimes we went by bus. No one asks questions when you're nobody special and you walk, like all the other African people themselves, or take the buses, that the whites never use; it's only if you've got the money for cars or to arrive at the airports that all these things happen that you read about: getting sent back over the border, refused permits, and so on. So we got here, to Tanganyika at last, down to this town of Dar es Salaam where we'd been told we'd be going.

There's a refugee camp here and they give you a shilling or two a day until you get work. But it's out of town, for one thing, and we soon left there and found a room down in the native town. There are some nice buildings, of course, in the real town – nothing like Johannesburg or Durban, though – and that used to be the white town, the whites who are left still live there, but the Africans with big jobs in the government and so on live there too. Some of our leaders who are refugees like us live in these houses and have big cars; everyone knows they're important men, here, not like at home where if you're black you're just rubbish for the Locations. The people down where we lived are very poor and it's hard to get work because they haven't got enough work for themselves, but I've got my standard seven and I managed to get a small job as a clerk. Josias never found steady work. But that didn't matter so much because the big thing was that Emma was able to come to join us after five months, and she and I earn the money. She's a nurse, you see, and Africanization started in the hospitals and the government was short of nurses. So Emma got the chance to come up with a party of them sent for specially from South Africa and Rhodesia. We were very lucky because it's impossible for people to get their families up here. She came in a plane paid for by the government, and she and the other girls had their photograph taken for the newspaper as they got off at the airport. That day she came we took her to the beach, where everyone can bathe, no restrictions, and for a cool drink in one of the hotels (she'd never been in a hotel before), and we walked up and down the road along the bay where everyone walks and where you can see the ships coming in and going out so near that the men out there wave to you. Whenever we bumped into anyone else from home they would stop and ask her about home, and how everything was. Josias and I couldn't stop grinning to hear us all, in the middle of Dar, talking away in our language about the things we know. That day it was like it had happened already: the time when we are home again and everything is our way.

Well, that's nearly three years ago, since Emma came. Josias has been sent away now and there's only Emma and me. That was always the idea, to send us away for training. Some go to Ethiopia and some go to Algeria and all over the show and by the time they come back there won't be anything Verwoerd's men know in the way of handling guns and so on that they won't know better. That's for a start. I'm supposed to go too, but some of us have been waiting a long time. In the meantime I go to work and I walk about this place in the evenings and I buy myself a glass of beer in a bar when I've got money. Emma and I have still got the flat we had before Josias left and two nurses from the hospital pay us for the other bedroom. Emma still works at the hospital but I don't know how much longer. Most days now since Josias's gone she wants me to walk up to fetch her from the hospital when she comes off duty, and when I get under the trees on the drive I see her staring out looking for me as if I'll never turn up ever again. Every day it's like that. When I come up she smiles and looks like she used to for a minute but by the time we're ten yards on the road she's shaking and shaking her head until the tears come, and saying over and over. 'A person can't stand it, a person can't stand it.' She said right from the beginning that the hospitals here are not like the hospitals at home, where the nurses have to know their job. She's got a whole ward in her charge and now she says they're worse and worse and she can't trust anyone to do anything for her. And the staff don't like having strangers working with them anyway. She tells me every day like she's telling me for the first time. Of course it's true that some of the people don't like us being here. You know how it is, people haven't got enough jobs to go round, themselves. But I don't take much notice; I'll be sent off one of these days and until then I've got to eat and that's that.

The flat is nice with a real bathroom and we are paying off the table and six chairs she liked so much, but when we walk in, her face is terrible. She keeps saying the place will never be straight. At home there was only a tap in the yard for all the houses but she never said it there. She doesn't sit down for more than a minute without getting up at once again, but you can't get her to go out, even on these evenings when it's so hot you can't breathe. I go down to the market to buy the food now, she says she can't stand it. When I asked why – because at the beginning she used to like the market, where you can pick a live fowl for yourself, quite cheap – she said those little rotten tomatoes they grow here, and dirty people all shouting and she can't understand. She doesn't sleep, half the time, at night, either, and lately she wakes me up. It happened only last night. She was standing there in the dark and she said, 'I felt bad.' I said, 'I'll make you some tea', though what good could tea do. 'There must be something the matter with me,' she says. 'I must go to the doctor tomorrow.'

'Is it pains again, or what?'

She shakes her head slowly, over and over, and I know she's going to cry again. 'A place where there's no one. I get up and look out the window and it's just like I'm not awake. And every day, every day. I can't ever wake up and be out of it. I always see this town.'

Of course it's hard for her. I've picked up Swahili and I can get around all right; I mean I can always talk to anyone if I feel like it, but she hasn't learnt more than *ahsante* – she could've picked it up just as easily, but she *can't*, if you know what I mean. It's just a noise to her, like dogs barking or those black crows in the palm trees. When anyone does come here to see her – someone else from home, usually, or perhaps I bring the Rhodesian who works where I do – she only sits there and whatever anyone talks about she doesn't listen until she can sigh and say, 'Heavy, heavy. Yes, for a woman alone. No friends, nobody. For a woman alone, I can tell you.'

Last night I said to her, 'It would be worse if you were at home, you wouldn't have seen Josias or me for a long time.'

But she said, 'Yes, it would be bad. Sela and everybody. And the old crowd at the hospital – but just the same, it would be bad. D'you remember how we used to go right into town on my Saturday off? The people – ay! Even when you were twelve you used to be scared you'd lose me.'

'I wasn't scared, you were the one was scared to get run over sometimes.' But in the Location when we stole fruit, and sweets

135

from the shops. Emma could always grab me out of the way of trouble, Emma always saved me. The same Emma. And yet it's not the same. And what could I do for her?

I suppose she wants to be back there now. But still she wouldn't be the same. I don't often get the feeling she knows what I'm thinking about, any more, or that I know what she's thinking, but she said, 'You and he go off, you come back or perhaps you don't come back, you know what you must do. But for a woman? What shall I do there in my life? What shall I do here? What time is this for a woman?'

It's hard for her. Emma. She'll say all that often now, I know. She tells me everything so many times. Well, I don't mind it when I fetch her from the hospital and I don't mind going to the market. But straight after we've eaten, now, in the evenings, I let her go through it once and then I'm off. To walk in the streets when it gets a bit cooler in the dark. I don't know why it is, but I'm thinking so bloody hard about getting out there in the streets that I push down my food as fast as I can without her noticing. I'm so keen to get going I feel queer, kind of tight and excited. Just until I can get out and not hear. I wouldn't even mind skipping the meal. In the streets in the evening everyone is out. On the grass along the bay the fat Indians in their white suits with their wives in those fancy coloured clothes. Men and their girls holding hands. Old watchmen like beggars, sleeping in the doorways of the shut shops. Up and down people walk, walk, just sliding one foot after the other because now and then, like somebody lifting a blanket, there's air from the sea. She should come out for a bit of air in the evening, man. It's an old, old place this, they say. Not the buildings, I mean; but the place. They say ships were coming here before even a place like London was a town. She thought the bay was so nice, that first day. The lights from the ships run all over the water and the palms show up a long time even after it gets dark. There's a smell I've smelled ever since we've been here – three years! I don't mean the smells in the native town; a special warm night-smell. You can even smell it at three in the morning. I've smelled it when I was standing about with Emma, by the window; it's as hot in the middle of the night here as it is in the middle of the day, at home – funny, when you look at the stars and the dark. Well, I'll be going off soon. It can't be long now. Now that Josias is gone. You've just got to wait your time; they haven't forgotten about you. Dar es Salaam. Dar. Sometimes I walk with another chap from home, he says some things, makes you laugh! He says the old watchmen who sleep in the doorways get their wives to come there with them. Well, I haven't seen it. He says we're definitely going with the next lot. Dar es Salaam. Dar. One day I suppose I'll remember it and tell my wife I stayed three years there, once. I walk and walk, along the bay, past the shops and hotels and the German church and the big bank, and through the mud streets between old shacks and stalls. It's dark there and full of other walking shapes as I wander past light coming from the cracks in the walls, where the people are in their homes.

Open House

F rances Taver was on the secret circuit for people who wanted to find out the truth about South Africa. These visiting journalists, politicians, and churchmen all had an itinerary arranged for them by their consular representatives and overseas information services, or were steered around by a 'foundation' of South African business interests eager to improve the country's image, or even carted about to the model black townships, universities and beerhalls by the South African State Information service itself. But all had, carefully hidden among the most private of private papers (the nervous ones went so far as to keep it in code), the short list that would really take the lid off the place: the people one must see. A few were names that had got into the newspapers of the world as particularly vigorous opponents or victims of apartheid; a writer or two, a newspaper editor or an outspoken bishop. Others were known only within the country itself, and were known about by foreign visitors only through people like themselves who had carried the short list before. Most of the names on it were white names – which was rather frustrating, when one was after the real thing; but it was said in London and New York that there *were* still ways of getting to meet Africans, provided you could get hold of the right white people.

Frances Taver was one of them. Had been for years. From the Forties when she had been a trade union organizer and run a mixed union of garment workers while this was legally possible, in the Fifties, after her marriage, when she was manager of a black-and-white theatre group before that was disbanded by new legislation, to the early Sixties, when she hid friends on the run from the police – Africans who were members of the newly-banned political organizations – before the claims of that sort of friendship had to be weighed against the risk of the long spells of detention without trial introduced to betray it.

Frances Taver had few friends left now, and she was always slightly embarrassed when she heard an eager American or English voice over the telephone, announcing an arrival, a too-brief stay (of course), and the inevitable fond message of greetings to be conveyed from so-and-so – whoever it was who happened to have supplied the short list. A few years ago it had been fun and easy to make these visitors an excuse for a gathering that quite likely would turn into a party. The visitor would have a high old time learning to dance the *kwela* with black girls; he would sit fascinated, trying to keep sober enough to take it all in, listening to the fluent and fervent harangue of African, white, and Indian politicals, drinking and arguing together in a paradox of personal freedom that, curiously, he couldn't remember finding where there were *no* laws against the mixing of races. And no one enjoyed his fascination more than the objects of it themselves; Frances Taver and her friends were amused, in those days, in a friendly way, to knock the 'right' ideas slightly askew. In those days: that was how she thought of it; it seemed very long ago. She saw the faces, sometimes, a flash in an absence filled with newspaper accounts of trials, hearsay about activities in exile, chance remarks from someone who knew someone else who had talked over the fence with one who was under house arrest. Another, an African friend banned for his activities with the African National Congress, who had gone 'underground', came to see her at long intervals, in the afternoons when he could be sure the house would be empty. Although she was still youngish, she had come to think of 'those days' as her youth, and he was a vision strayed from it.

The voice on the telephone, this time, was American – soft, cautious – no doubt the man thought the line was tapped. Robert Greenman Ceretti, from Washington; while they were talking, she remembered that this was the political columnist who had somehow been connected with the Kennedy administration. Hadn't he written a book about the Bay of Pigs? Anyway, she had certainly seen him quoted.

'And how are the Brauns – I haven't heard for ages – ' She made the usual inquiries about the well-being of the mutual acquaintance whose greetings he brought, and he made the usual speech about how much he was hoping he'd be able to meet her? She was about to say, as always, come to dinner, but an absurd recoil within her, a moment of dull panic, almost, made her settle for an invitation to drop in for a drink two days later. 'If I can be of any help to you, in the meantime?' she had to add; he sounded modest and intelligent.

'Well, I do appreciate it. I'll look forward to Wednesday.'

At the last minute she invited a few white friends to meet him, a doctor and his wife who ran a tuberculosis hospital in an African reserve, and a young journalist who had been to America on a leadership exchange programme. But she knew what the foreign visitor wanted of her and she had an absurd – again, that was the word – compulsion to put him in the position where, alas, he could ask it. He was a small, cosy, red-headed man with a chipmunk smile, and she liked him. She drove him back to his hotel after the other guests had left, and they chatted about the articles he was going to write and the people he was seeing – had he been able to interview any important Nationalists, for example? Well, not yet, but he hoped to have something lined up for the following week, in Pretoria. Another thing he was worried about (here it came), he'd hardly been able to exchange a word with any black man except the one who cleaned his room at the hotel. She heard her voice saying casually, 'Well, perhaps I might be able to help you, there', and he took it up at once, gravely, gratefully, sincerely, smiling at her – 'I hoped you just might. If I could only get to talk with a few ordinary, articulate people I mean, I think I've been put pretty much in the picture by the courageous white people I've been lucky enough to meet – people like you and your husband – but I'd like to know a little at first-hand about what Africans themselves are thinking. If you could fix it, it'd be wonderful.'

Now it was done, at once she withdrew, from herself rather than him. 'I don't know. People don't want to talk any more. If they're doing anything, it's not something that can be talked about. Those that are left. Black and white. The ones you ought to see are shut away.'

They were sitting in the car, outside the hotel. She could see in his encouraging, admiring, intent face how he had been told that she, if anyone, could introduce him to black people, hers, if anyone's, was the house to meet them.

There was a twinge of vanity: 'I'll let you know. I'll ring you, then, Bob.' Of course they were already on first-name terms; lonely affinity overleapt acquaintance in South Africa when like-minded whites met.

'You don't have to say more than when and where. I didn't like to talk, that first day, over the phone,' he said.

They always had fantasies of danger. 'What can happen to you?' she said. Her smile was not altogether pleasant. They always protested, too, that their fear was not for themselves, it was on your behalf, etc. 'You've got your passport. You don't live here.'

She did not see Jason Madela from one month's end to the next but when she telephoned him at the building where she remembered him once having had an office on the fringe of the white town, he accepted the invitation to lunch just as if he had been one of the intimates who used to drop in any time. And then there was Edgar, Edgar Xixo the attorney, successor to her old friend Samson Dumile's practice, one could always get him. And after that? She could have asked Jason to bring someone along, perhaps one of the boxing promoters or gamblers it amused him to produce where the drinks were free – but that would have been too obvious, even for the blind eye that she and Jason Madela were able to turn to the nature of the invitation. In the end she invited little Spuds Butelezi, the reporter. What did it matter? He was black, anyway. There was no getting out of the whole business, now.

She set herself to cook a good lunch, just as good as she had ever cooked, and she put out the drinks and the ice in the shelter of the glassed-in end of the big veranda, so that the small company should not feel lost. Her fading hair had been dyed to something approximating its original blonde and then streaked with grey, the day before, and she felt the appearance to be pleasingly artificial; she wore a bright, thick linen dress that showed off sunburned shoulders like the knobs of well-polished furniture, and she was aware that her blue eyes were striking in contrast with her tough brown face. She felt Robert Greenman Ceretti's eyes on her, a moment, as he stood in the sunny doorway; yes, she was also a woman, queening it alone among men at lunch. 'You mix

141

the martinis, there's a dear,' she said. 'It's such a treat to have a real American one.' And while he bent about over bottles with the neatness of a small man, she was in and out of the veranda, shepherding the arrival of the other guests. 'This is Bob – Bob Ceretti, here on a visit from the States – Edgar Xixo.'

'Jason, this is Bob Ceretti, the man who has the ear of presidents—'

Laughter and protests mingled with the handing round of the drinks. Jason Madela, going to fat around the nape but still handsome in a frowning, Clark Gable way, stood about glass in hand as if in the habit acquired at cocktail parties. With his air of being distracted from more important things by irresistibly amusing asides, he was correcting a matter of terminology for Robert Ceretti – 'No, no, but you must understand that in the townships, a "situation" is a different thing entirely – well, *I'm* a situation, f'rinstance—' He cocked his smile, for confirmation, to Xixo, whose eyes turned from one face to another in obedient glee – 'Oh, you're the *muti* man!' 'No, wait, but I'm trying to give Bob an obvious example' – more laughter, all round – '– a man who wears a suit every day, like a white man. Who goes to the office and prefers to talk English.'

'You think it derives from the use of the word as a genteelism for "job"? Would you say? You know – the Situations Vacant column in the newspapers?' The visitor sat forward on the edge of his chair, smiling up closely. 'But what's this *"muti"* you mentioned, now – maybe I ought to have been taking notes instead of shaking Frances' martini pitcher.'

'He's a medicine man', Xixo was explaining, while Jason laughed – 'Oh for God's sake!' and tossed off the rest of his gin, and Frances went forward to bring the late arrival, Spuds Butelezi, in his lattice-knit gold shirt and pale blue jeans, into the circle. When the American had exchanged names and had Spuds by the hand, he said, 'And what's Spuds, then?'

The young man had a dough-shaped, light-coloured face with tiny features stuck in it in a perpetual expression of suspicious surprise. The martinis had turned up the volume of voices that met him. 'I'll have a beer', he said to Frances; and they laughed again.

Jason Madela rescued him, a giant flicking a fly from a glass of water. 'He's one of the egg-heads,' he said. 'That's another category altogether.'

'Didn't you used to be one yourself, Jason?' Frances pretended a reproof: Jason Madela would want a way of letting Ceretti know that although he was a successful business man in the townships, he was also a man with a university degree.

'Don't let's talk about my youthful misdemeanours, my dear Frances,' he said, with the accepted light touch of a man hiding a wound. 'I thought the men were supposed to be doing the work around here – I can cope with that' and he helped her chip apart the ice-cubes that had welded together as they melted. 'Get your servant to bring us a little hot water, that'll do it easily—'

'Oh I'm really falling down on the job!' Ceretti was listening carefully, putting on a low 'Go on' or 'You mean?' to keep the flow of Xixo's long explanation of problems over a travel document, and he looked up at Frances and Jason Madela offering a fresh round of drinks.

'You go ahead and talk, that's the idea,' Frances said.

He gave her the trusting grin of some intelligent small pet. 'Well, you two are a great combination behind the bar. Real teamwork of long association, I guess.'

'How long is it?' Frances asked, drily but gaily, meaning how many years had she and Jason Madela been acquaintances, and, playfully making as if to anticipate a blow, he said, 'Must be ten years and you were a grown-up girl even then' – although both knew that they had seen each other only across various rooms perhaps a dozen times in five years, and got into conversation perhaps half as often.

At lunch Edgar Xixo was still fully launched on the story of his difficulties in travelling back and forth to one of the former British Protectorates, now small, newly independent states surrounded by South African territory. It wasn't, he explained, as if he were asking for a passport: it was just a travel document he wanted, that's all, just a piece of paper from the Bantu Affairs Department that would allow him to go to Lesotho on business and come back.

'Now have I got this straight – you'd been there sometime?' Ceretti hung over the wisp of steam rising from his soup like a seer over a crystal ball.

'Yes, yes, you see, I had a travel document—'

'But these things are good for one exit and re-entry only.' Jason dispatched it with the good-humoured impatience of the quick-witted. 'We blacks aren't supposed to want to go wandering about the place. Tell them you want to take a holiday in Lourenço Marques – they'll laugh in your face. If they don't kick you down-stairs. Oppenheimer and Charlie Engelhard can go off in their yachts to the South of France, but Jason Madela?'

He got the laugh he wanted, and, on the side, the style of his reference to rich and important white industrialists as decent enough fellows, if one happened to know them, suggested that *he* might. Perhaps he did, for all Frances Taver knew; Jason would be just the kind of man the white establishment would find if they should happen to decide they ought to make a token gesture of being in touch with the African masses. He was curiously reassur-ing to white people, his dark suits, white shirts, urbane conversa-tion and sense of humour, all indistinguishable from their own and apparently snatched out of thin air, made it possible for them to forget the unpleasant facts of the life imposed on him and his kind. How tactful, how clever he was, too. She, just as well as any millionaire, would have done to illustrate his point; she was culpable; white, and free to go where she pleased. The flattery of being spared passed invisibly from her to him, like a promissory note beneath the table.

Edgar Xixo had even been summoned to The Greys, Special Branch headquarters, for questioning, he said – 'And I've never belonged to any political organization, they know there've never been any charges against me. I don't know any political refugees in Lesotho, I don't want to *see* anybody – I have to go up and down simply because of business, I've got this agency selling equipment to the people at the diamond diggings, it could be a good thing if . . .'

'A little palm-grease, maybe', said Jason Madela, taking some salad.

Xixo appealed to them all, dismayed. 'But if you offer it to the wrong one, that's the . . . In my position, an attorney!'

'Instinct,' said Madela. 'One can't learn it.'

'Tell me,' Ceretti signalled an appreciative refusal of a second helping of duck, while turning from his hostess to Madela. 'Would

144

you say that bribery plays a big part in daily relations between Africans and officials? I don't mean the political police, of course – the white administration? Is that your experience?'

Madela sipped his wine and then turned the bottle so that he could read the label, saying meanwhile, 'Oh not what you'd call graft, not by your standards. Small stuff. When I ran a transport business I used to make use of it. Licences for the drivers and so on. You get some of these young Afrikaner clerks, they don't earn much and they don't mind who they pick up a few bob from. They can be quite reasonable. I was thinking there might be someone up at the Bantu Affairs offices. But you have to have a feeling for the right man' – he put down the bottle and smiled at Frances Taver – 'Thank heaven I'm out of it, now. Unless I should decide to submit some of my concoctions to the Bureau of Standards, eh?' and she laughed.

'Jason has broken the white monopoly of the hair-straightener and blood-purifier business,' Frances said gracefully, 'and the nice thing about him is that he has no illusions about his products.'

'But plenty of confidence,' he said. 'I'm looking into the possibilities of exporting my pills for men, to the States. I think the time's just ripe for American Negroes to feel they can buy back a bit of old Africa in a bottle, eh?'

Xixo picked about his leg of duck as if his problem itself were laid cold before them on the table. 'I mean, I've said again and again, show me anything on my record—'

The young journalist, Spuds Butelezi, said in his heavy way, 'It might be because you took over Samson Dumile's show.'

Every time a new name was mentioned the corners of Ceretti's eyes flickered narrow in attention.

'Well, that's the whole thing!' Xixo complained to Ceretti. 'The fellow I was working for, Dumile, was mixed up in a political trial and he got six years – I took over the *bona fide* clients, that's all, my office isn't in the same building, nothing to do with it – but that's the whole thing!'

Frances suddenly thought of Sam Dumile, in this room of hers, three – two? – years ago, describing a police raid on his house the night before and roaring with laughter as he told how his little daughter said to the policeman. 'My father gets very cross if you play with his papers.'

Jason picked up the wine bottle, making to pass it round – 'Yes, please do, please do – what happened to the children?' she said. Jason knew whose she meant, made a polite attempt. 'Where are Sam's kids?'

But Edgar Xixo was nodding in satisfied confirmation as Ceretti said, 'It's a pretty awful story. My God. Seems you can never hope to be in the clear, no matter how careful you are. My God.'

Jason remarked, aside. 'They must be around somewhere with relatives. He's got a sister in Bloemfontein.'

The dessert was a compound of fresh mangoes and cream, an invention of the house: '*Mangoes Frances*' said the American. 'This is one of the African experiences I'd recommend.' But Jason Madela told them he was allergic to mangoes and began on the cheese which was standing by. Another bottle of wine was opened to go with the cheese and there was laughter – which Robert Ceretti immediately turned on himself – when it emerged out of the cross-talk that Spuds Butelezi thought Ceretti had something to do with an American foundation. In the sympathetic atmosphere of food, drink, and sunshine marbled with cigarette smoke, the others listened as if they had not heard it all before while Butelezi, reluctant to waste the speech he had primed himself with, pressed Ceretti with his claim to a study grant that would enable him to finish his play. They heard him again outlining the plot and inspiration of the play – 'right out of township life' as he always said, blinking with finality, convinced that this was the only necessary qualification for successful authorship. He had patiently put together and taken apart, many times, in his play, ingredients faithfully lifted from the work of African writers who got published, and he was himself African: what else could be needed but someone to take it up?

Foundation or no foundation, Robert Ceretti showed great interest. 'Do you know the play at all, Frances? I mean' (he turned back to the round, wine-open face of the young man) 'is it far enough along to show to anybody?' And she said, finding herself smiling encouragingly. 'Oh, yes – an early draft, he's worked on it a lot since then haven't you – and there's been a reading . . .?'

'I'll certainly get it to you', Butelezi said, writing down the name of Ceretti's hotel.

They moved back to the veranda for the coffee and brandy. It was well after three o'clock by the time they stood about, making their good-byes. Ceretti's face was gleaming. 'Jason Madela's offered to drop me back in town, so don't you worry, Frances. I was just saying, people in America'll find it difficult to believe it was possible for me to have a lunch like this, here. It's been so very pleasant – pleasant indeed. We all had a good time. He was telling me that a few years ago a gathering like this would be quite common, but now there aren't many white people who would want to risk asking Africans and there aren't many Africans who would risk coming. I certainly enjoyed myself . . . I hope we haven't put you out, lingering so long . . . It's been a wonderful opportunity . . .' Frances saw them to the garden gate, talking and laughing; last remarks and good-byes were called from under the trees of the suburban street.

When she came back alone the quiet veranda rang tense with vanished voices, like a bell tower after the hour has struck. She gave the cat the milk left over from coffee. Someone had left a half-empty packet of cigarettes; who was it who broke matches into little tents? As she carried the tray into the deserted kitchen, she saw a note written on the back of a bill taken from the spike. HOPE YOUR PARTY WENT WELL.

It was not signed, and was written with the kitchen ball-point which hung on a string. But she knew who had written it; the vision from the past had come up from 'underground', come and gone again.

The servants Amos and Bettie had rooms behind a granadilla vine at the bottom of the yard. She called, and asked Bettie whether anyone had asked for her? No, no one at all.

The African Congress man must have heard the voices in the quiet of the afternoon, or perhaps simply seen the cars outside, and gone away. She wondered if he knew who was there. Had he gone away out of consideration for her safety? They never spoke of it, of course, but he must know that the risks she took were carefully calculated. very carefully calculated. There was no way of disguising that from someone like *him*. Then she saw him smiling to himself at the sight of the collection of guests: Jason Madela, Edgar Xixo, and Spuds Butelezi – Spuds Butelezi, as well. But probably she was wrong, and he would have come out among them without those feelings of reproach or contempt that she read

147

into the idea of his gait, his face. HOPE YOUR PARTY WENT WELL. He may have meant just that.

Frances Taver knew Robert Ceretti was leaving soon, but she wasn't quite sure when. Every day she thought; I'll phone and say good-bye. Yet she had already taken leave of him, that afternoon of the lunch. Just telephone and say good-bye. On the Friday morning, when she was sure he would be gone, she rang up the hotel, and there it was, the soft, cautious American voice. The first few moments were awkward; he protested his pleasure at hearing from her, she kept repeating, 'I thought you'd be gone . . .' Then she said, 'I just wanted to say – about that lunch. You mustn't be taken in—' He was saying. 'I've been so indebted to you, Frances, really, you've been great.'

'—not phonies, no, that's not what I mean, on the contrary, they're very real, you understand?'

'Oh, your big good-looking friend, he's been marvellous. Saturday night we were out on the town, you know.' He was proud of the adventure but didn't want to use the word '*shebeen*' over the telephone.

She said, 'You must understand. Because the corruption's real. Even they've become what they are because things are the way they are. Being phony is being corrupted by the situation . . . and that's real enough. We're made out of *that*.'

He thought maybe he was finding it difficult to follow her over the telephone, and seized upon the word. 'Yes, the "situation" – he was able to slip me into what I gather is one of the livelier places.'

Frances Taver said, 'I don't want you to be taken in—'

The urgency of her voice stopped his mouth, was communicated to him even if what she said was not.

'—by anyone', the woman was saying.

He understood, indeed, that something complicated was wrong, but he knew, too, that he wouldn't be there long enough to find out, that perhaps you needed to live and die there, to find out. All she heard over the telephone was the voice assuring her, 'Everyone's been marvellous . . . really marvellous. I just hope I can get back here some day – that is, if they ever let me in again . . .'

Africa Emergent

H e's in prison now, so I'm not going to mention his name. It mightn't be a good thing, you understand. – Perhaps you think you understand too well; but don't be quick to jump to conclusions from five or six thousand miles away: if you lived here, you'd understand something else – friends know that shows of loyalty are all right for children holding hands in the school playground; for us they're luxuries, not important and maybe dangerous. If I said, I was a friend of so-and-so, black man awaiting trial for treason, what good would it do him? And, who knows, it might draw just that decisive bit more attention to me. *He*'d be the first to agree.

Not that one feels that if they haven't got enough in my dossier already, this would make any difference; and not that he really was such a friend. But that's something else you won't understand; everything is ambiguous, here. We hardly know, by now, what we can do and what we can't do; it's difficult to say, goaded in on oneself by laws and doubts and rebellion and caution and – not least – self-disgust, what is or is not a friendship. I'm talking about black-and-white, of course. If you stay with it, boy, on the white side in the country clubs and garden suburbs if you're white, and on the black side in the locations and beerhalls if you're black, none of this applies, and you can go all the way to your segregated cemetery in peace. But neither he nor I did.

I began mixing with blacks out of what is known as an outraged sense of justice, plus strong curiosity, when I was a student. There were two ways – one was through the white students' voluntary service organization, a kibbutz-type junket where white boys and girls went into rural areas and camped while they built school classrooms for African children. A few coloured and African

149

students from their segregated universities used to come along, too, and there was the novelty, not without value, of dossing down alongside them at night, although we knew we were likely to be harbouring Special Branch spies among our willing workers, and we dared not make a pass at the coloured or black girls. The other way – less hard on the hands – was to go drinking with the jazz musicians and journalists, painters and would-be poets and actors who gravitated towards whites partly because such people naturally feel they can make free of the world, and partly because they found an encouragement and appreciation there that was sweet to them. I tried the VSO briefly, but the other way suited me better; anyway, I didn't see why I should help this Government by doing the work it ought to be doing for the welfare of black children.

I'm an architect and the way I was usefully drawn into the black scene was literally that: I designed sets for a mixed colour drama group got together by a white director. Perhaps there's no urban human group as intimate, in the end, as a company of this kind, and the colour problem made us even closer. I don't mean what *you* mean, the how-do-I-feel-about-that-black-skin stuff; I mean the daily exasperation of getting round, or over, or on top of the colour bar laws that plagued our productions and our lives. We had to remember to write out 'passes' at night, so that our actors could get home without being arrested for being out after the curfew for blacks, we had to spend hours at the Bantu Affairs Department trying to arrange local residence permits for actors who were being 'endorsed out' of town back to the villages to which, 'ethnically', apparently, they belonged although they'd never set eyes on them, and we had to decide which of us could play the sycophant well enough to persuade the Bantu Commissioner to allow the show to go on the road from one Group Area, designated by colour, to another, or to talk some town clerk into getting his council to agree to the use of a 'white' public hall by a mixed cast. The black actors' lives were in our hands, because they were black and we were white, and could, must, intercede for them. Don't think this made everything love and light between us, in fact it caused endless huffs and rows. A white woman who'd worked like a slave acting as P R O-cum wardrobe-mistress hasn't spoken to me for years because I made her lend her little car to one of the chaps who'd worked until after the last train went back to the location, and then he kept it the whole weekend and she couldn't get hold of him because, of course, location houses rarely have telephones and once a black man has disappeared among those warrens you won't find him till he chooses to surface in the white town again. And when this one did surface, he was biting, to me, about white bitches' 'patronage' of people they secretly still thought of as 'boys'. Yet our arguments, resentments and mis-understandings were not only as much part of the intimacy of this group as the good times, the parties and the love-making we had, but were more – the defining part, because we'd got close enough to admit argument, resentment and misunderstanding between us.

He was one of this little crowd, for a time. He was a dispatch clerk and then a 'manager' and chucker-out at a black dance club. In his spare time he took a small part in our productions now and then, and made himself generally handy; in the end it was discovered that what he really was good at was front-of-house arrangements. His tubby charm (he was a large young man and a cheerful dresser) was just the right thing to deal with the un-expected moods of our location audiences when we went on tour – sometimes they came stiffly encased in their church-going best and seemed to feel it was vulgar to laugh or respond to what was going on, on stage; in other places they rushed the doors, tried to get in without paying, and were dominated by a *tsotsi*, street urchin, element who didn't want to hear anything but themselves. He was the particular friend – the other, passive half – of a particu-lar friend of mine, Elias Nkomo.

And here I stop short. How shall I talk about Elias? I've never even learnt, in five years, how to think about him.

Elias was a sculptor. He had one of those jobs – messenger 'boy' or some such – that literate young black men can aspire to in a small gold-mining and industrial town outside Johannesburg. Somebody said he was talented, somebody sent him to me – at the beginning, the way for every black man to find himself seems inescapably to lead through a white man. Again, how can I say what his work was like? He came by train to the black people's section of Johannesburg central station, carrying a bulky object wrapped in that morning's newspaper. He was slight, round-headed, tiny-eared, dunly dressed, and with a frown of effort between his eyes, but his face unfolded to a wide, apologetic yet confident smile when he realized that the white man in a waiting car must be me – the meeting had been arranged. I took him back to my 'place' (he always called people's homes that) and he unwrapped the newspaper. What was there was nothing like the clumps of diorite or sandstone you have seen in galleries in New York, London, or Johannesburg marked 'Africa Emergent', 'Spirit of the Ancestors'. What was there was a goat, or a goat-like creature, in the way that a centaur is a horse-like, man-like creature, carved out of streaky knotted wood. It was delightful (I wanted to put out my hand to touch it), it was moving in its somehow concretized diachrony, beast-man, coarse wood – fine workmanship, and there was also something exposed about it (one would withdraw the hand, after all). I asked him whether he knew Picasso's goats? He had heard of Picasso but never seen any of his work. I showed him a photograph of the famous bronze goat in Picasso's own house; thereafter all his beasts had sex organs as joyful as Picasso's goat's udder, but that was the only 'influence' that ever took, with him. As I say, a white man always intercedes in some way, with a man like Elias; mine was to keep him from those art-loving ladies with galleries who wanted to promote him, and those white painters and sculptors who were willing to have him work under their tutelage. I gave him an old garage (well, that means I took my car out of it) and left him alone, with plenty of chunks of wood.

But Elias didn't like the loneliness of work. That garage never became his 'place'. Perhaps when you've lived in an overcrowded yard all your life the counter-stimulus of distraction becomes necessary to create a tension of concentration. No – well all I really mean is that he liked company. At first he came only at weekends, and then, as he began to sell some of his work, he gave up the messenger job and moved in more or less permanently – we fixed up the 'place' together, putting in a ceiling and connecting water and so on. It was illegal for him to live there in a white suburb of course, but such laws breed complementary evasions in people like Elias and me and the white building inspector didn't turn a hair of suspicion when I said that I was converting the garage as a flat for my wife's mother. It was better for Elias once he'd moved in: there was always some friend of his sharing his bed, not to mention the girls who did; sometimes the girls were shy little things almost of the kitchenmaid variety, who called my wife 'madam' when they happened to bump into her, crossing the garden, sometimes they were the bewigged and painted actresses from the group who sat smoking and gossiping with my wife while she fed the baby.

And *he* was there more often than anyone – the plump and cheerful front-of-house manager; he was married, but as happens with our sex, an old friendship was a more important factor in his life than a wife and kids – if that's a characteristic of black men, then I must be black under the skin, myself. Elias had become very involved in the theatre group, anyway, like *him*; Elias made some beautiful *papier mâché* gods for a play by a Nigerian that we did – 'spirits of the ancestors' at once amusing and frightening – and once when we needed a singer he surprisingly turned out to have a voice that could phrase a madrigal as easily as whatever the forerunner of Soul was called – I forget now, but it blared hour after hour from the garage when he was working. Elias seemed to like best to work when the other one was around; *he* would sit with his fat boy's legs rolled out before him, flexing his toes in his fashionable shoes, dusting down the lapels of the latest thing in jackets, as he changed the records and kept up a monologue contentedly punctuated by those soft growls and sighs of agreement, those sudden squeezes of almost silent laughter – responses possible only in an African language – that came from Elias as he chiselled and chipped. For they spoke in their own tongue, and I have never known what it was they talked about.

In spite of my efforts to let him alone, inevitably Elias was 'taken up' (hadn't I started the process myself, with that garage?) and a gallery announced itself his agent. He walked about at the opening of his one-man show in a purple turtle-necked sweater I think his best friend must have made him buy, laughing a little, softly, at himself, more embarrassed than pleased. An art critic wrote about his transcendental values and plastic modality, and he said, 'Christ, man, does he dig it or doesn't he?' while we toasted his success in brandy chased with beer – brandy isn't a rich man's sip in South Africa, it's made here and it's what people use to get drunk on. He earned quite a bit of money that year. Then the gallery owner and the art critic forgot him in the discovery of yet another interpreter of the African soul, and he was poor again, but he had acquired a patroness who, although she lived far away, did not forget him. She was, as you might have thought, an American lady, very old and wealthy according to South African legend but probably simply a middle-aged widow with comfortable stock holdings and a desire to get in on the cultural ground floor of some form of art collecting not yet overcrowded. She had bought some of his work while a tourist in Johannesburg. Perhaps she did have academic connections with the art world; in any case, it was she who got a foundation to offer Elias Nkomo a scholarship to study in America.

I could understand that he wanted to go simply in order to go: to see the world outside. But I couldn't believe that at this stage he wanted or could make use of formal art school disciplines. As I said to him at the time, I'm only an architect, but I've had experience of the academic and even, God help us, the frenziedly non-academic approach in the best schools, and it's not for people who have, to fall back on the jargon, found themselves.

I remember he said, smiling, 'You think I've found myself?'

And I said, 'But you've never been lost, man. That very first goat wrapped in newspaper was your goat.'

But later, when he was refused a passport and the issue of his going abroad was much on our minds, we talked again. He wanted to go because he felt he needed some kind of general education, general cultural background that he'd missed, in his six years at the location school. 'Since I've been at your place, I've been reading a lot of your books. And man, I know nothing. I'm as ignorant as that kid of yours there in the pram. Right, I've picked up a bit of politics, a few art terms here and there – I can wag my head and say "plastic values" all right, eh? But man, what do I know about life? What do I know about how it all works? How do I know *how* I do the work I do? Why we live and die – If I carry on here I might as well be carving walking sticks', he added. I knew what he meant: there are old men, all over Africa, who make a living squatting at a decent distance from tourist hotels, carving fancy walking sticks from local wood; only one step in sophistication below the 'Africa Emergent' school of sculptors so rapturously acclaimed by gallery owners. We both laughed at this, and following the line of thought suggested to me by his question to himself: 'How do I know how I do the work I do?' – although in me it was a different line of thought from his – I asked him whether in fact there was any sort of traditional skill in his family? As I imagined, there was not – he was an urban slum kid, brought up opposite a municipal beerhall among paraffin-tin utensils and abandoned motor-car bodies which, perhaps curiously, had failed to bring out a Duchamp in him but from which, on the contrary, he had sprung, full-blown, as a classical expressionist. Although there were no rural walking-stick carvers in his ancestry, he did tell me something I had no idea would have been part of the experience of a location childhood – he had been sent, in his teens, to a tribal initiation school in the bush, and been circumcised according to rite. He described the experience vividly.

Once all attempts to get him a passport had failed. Elias's desire to go to America became something else, of course: an obsessive resentment against confinement itself. Inevitably, he was given no reason for the refusal. The official answer was the usual one – that it was 'not in the public interest' to reveal the reason for such things. Was it because 'they' had got to know he was 'living like a white man'? (Theory put to me by one of the black actors in the group.) Was it because a critic had dutifully described his work as expressive of the 'agony of the emergent African soul'? Nobody knew. Nobody ever knows. It is enough to be black; blacks are meant to stay put, in their own ethnically apportioned streets in their own segregated areas, in those parts of South Africa where the government says they belong. Yet – the whole way our lives are manœuvred, as I say, is an unanswered question – Elias's best friend suddenly got a passport. I hadn't even realized that *he* had been offered a scholarship or a study grant or something, too, *he* was invited to go to New York to study production and the latest acting techniques (it was the time of the Method rather than Grotowski). And *he* got a passport, 'first try' as Elias said with ungrudging pleasure and admiration; when someone black got a passport, then, there was a collective sense of pleasure in having outwitted we didn't quite know what. So they went together, *he* on his passport, and Elias Nkomo on an exit permit.

An exit permit is a one-way ticket, anyway. When you are granted one at your request but at the government's pleasure, you sign an undertaking that you will never return to South Africa

155

or its mandatory territory, South West Africa. You pledge this with signature and thumb-print. Elias Nkomo never came back. At first he wrote (and he wrote quite often) enthusiastically about the world outside that he had gained, and he seemed to be enjoying some kind of small vogue, not so much as a sculptor as a genuine, real live African Negro who was sophisticated enough to be asked to comment on this and that: the beauty of American women, life in Harlem or Watts, Black power as seen through the eyes, etc. He sent cuttings from *Ebony* and even from *The New York Times Magazine*. He said that a girl at *Life* was trying to get them to run a piece on his work; his work? – well, he hadn't settled down to anything new, yet, but the art centre was a really swinging place, Christ, the things people were doing, there! There were silences, naturally; we forgot about him and he forgot about us for weeks on end. Then the local papers picked up the sort of news they are alert to from all over the world. Elias Nkomo had spoken at an anti-apartheid rally. Elias Nkomo, in West African robes, was on the platform with Stokely Carmichael. 'Well, why not? He hasn't got to worry about keeping his hands clean for the time when he comes back home, has he?' – My wife was bitter in his defence. Yes, but I was wondering about his work – 'Will they leave him alone to work?' I didn't write to him, but it was as if my silence were read by him: a few months later I received a cutting from some university art magazine devoting a number to Africa, and there was a photograph of one of Elias's wood sculptures, with his handwriting along the margin of the page – *I know you don't think much of people who don't turn out new stuff but some people here seem to think this old thing of mine is good*. It was the sort of wry remark that, spoken aloud to me in the room, would have made us both laugh. I smiled, and meant to write. But within two weeks Elias was dead. He drowned himself early one morning in the river of the New England town where the art school was.

It was like the refusal of the passport; none of us knew why. In the usual arrogance one has in the face of such happenings, I even felt guilty about the letter. Perhaps, if one were thousands of miles from one's own 'place', in some sort of a bad way, just a small thing like a letter, a word of encouragement from someone who had hurt by being rather niggardly with encouragement in the past . . . ? And what pathetic arrogance, at that! As if the wisp of a letter, written by someone between other preoccupations, and in substance an encouraging lie (how splendid that your old work is receiving recognition in some piddling little magazine) could be anything round which the hand of a man going down for the second time might close. Because before Elias went under in that river he must have been deep in forlorn horrors about which I knew nothing, nothing. When people commit suicide they do so apparently out of some sudden self-knowledge that those of us, the living, do not have the will to acquire. That's what's meant by despair, isn't it – what they have come to know? And that's what one means when one says in extenuation of oneself, *I knew so little about him, really*. I knew Elias only in the self that he had presented at my 'place'; why, how out of place it had been, once, when he happened to mention that as a boy he had spent weeks in the bush with his circumcision group! Of course we – his friends – decided out of the facts we knew and our political and personal attitudes, why he had died: and perhaps it is true that he was sick to death, in the real sense of the phrase that has been forgotten, sick unto death with homesickness for the native land that had shut him out forever and that he was forced to conjure up for himself in the parody of 'native' dress that had nothing to do with his part of the continent, and the shame that a new kind of black platform-solidarity forced him to feel for his old dependence, in South Africa, on the friendship of white people. It was the South African government who killed him, it was culture shock – but perhaps neither our political bitterness nor our glibness with fashionable phrases can come near what combination of forces, within and without, led him to the fatal baptism of that early morning. *It is not in the private interest that this should be revealed*. Elias never came home. That's all.

But his best friend did, towards the end of that year. *He* came to see me after he had been in the country some weeks – I'd heard he was back. The theatre group had broken up; it seemed to be that, chiefly, he'd come to talk to me about: he wanted to know if there was any money left in the kitty for him to start up a small theatrical venture of his own, he was eager to use the know-how (his phrase) he'd learned in the States. He was really plump now and he wore the most extraordinary clothes. A Liberace jacket.

157

Plastic boots. An Afro wig that looked as if it had been made out of a bit of karakul from South West Africa. I teased him about it – we were at least good enough friends for that – asking him if he'd really been with the guerrillas instead of Off-Broadway? (There was a trial on at home, at the time, of South African political refugees who had tried to 'infiltrate' through South West Africa.) And felt slightly ashamed of my patronage of his taste when he said with such good humour, 'It's just a fun thing, man, isn't it great?' I was too cowardly to bring the talk round to the point: Elias. And when it couldn't be avoided I said the usual platitudes and he shook his head at them – 'Hell, man', and we fell silent. Then he told me that that was how he had got back – because Elias was dead, on the unused portion of Elias's air ticket. *His* study grant hadn't included travel expenses and he'd had to pay his own way over. So he'd had only a one-way ticket, but Elias's scholarship had included a return fare to the student's place of origin. It had been difficult to get the airline to agree to the transfers, he'd had to go to the scholarship foundation people, but they'd been very decent about fixing it for him.

He had told me all this so guilelessly that I was one of the people who became angrily indignant when the rumour began to go around that he was a police agent: who else would have the cold nerve to come back on a dead man's ticket, a dead man who couldn't ever have used that portion of the ticket himself, because he had taken an exit permit? And who could believe the story, anyway? Obviously, *he* had to find some way of explaining why he, a black man like any other, could travel freely back and forth between South Africa and other countries. He had a passport, hadn't he? Well, there you were. Why should *he* get a passport? What black man these days had a passport?

Yes, I was angry, and defended him, by proof of the innocence of the very naïveté with which – a black man, yes, and therefore used to the necessity of salvaging from disaster all his life, unable to afford the nice squeamishness of white men's delicacy – he took over Elias's air ticket because he was alive and needed it, as he might have taken up Elias's coat against the cold. I refused to avoid him, the way some members of the remnant of our group made it clear they did now, and I remained stony-faced outside the complicity of those knowing half-smiles that accompanied the mention of his name. We had never been close friends, of course, but he would turn up from time to time. He could not find theatrical work and had a job as a travelling salesman in the locations. He took to bringing three or four small boys along when he visited us; they were very subdued and whisperingly well-behaved and well-dressed in miniature suits – our barefoot children stared at them in awe. They were his children plus the children of the family he was living with, we gathered. He and I talked mostly about his difficulties – his old car was unreliable, his wife had left him, his commissions were low, and he could have taken up an offer to join a Chicago repertory company if he could have raised the fare to go back to America – while my wife fed ice-cream and cake to the silent children, or my children dutifully placed them one by one on the garden swing. We had begun to be able to talk about Elias's death. He had told me how, in the weeks before he died, Elias would get the wrong way on the moving stairway going down in the subway in New York and keep walking, walking up. 'I thought he was foolin' around, man, you know? Jus' climbin' those stairs and goin' noplace?'

He clung nostalgically to the American idiom; no African talks about 'noplace' when he means 'nowhere'. But he had abandoned the Afro wig and when we got talking about Elias he would hold his big, well-shaped head with its fine, shaven covering of his own wool propped between his hands as if in an effort to think more clearly about something that would never come clear; I felt suddenly at one with him in that gesture, and would say, 'Go on'. He would remember another example of how Elias had been 'acting funny' before he died. It was on one of those afternoon visits he said, 'And I don't think I ever told you about the business with the students at the college? How that last weekend – before he did it, I mean – he went around and invited everybody to a party, I dunno, a kind of feast he said it was. Some of them said he said a barbecue – you know what that is, same as a *braaivleis*, eh? But one of the others told me afterwards that he'd told them he was going to give them a real African feast, he was going to show them how the country people do it here at home when somebody gets married or there's a funeral or so. He wanted to know where he could buy a goat.'

'A goat?'

'That's right. A live goat. He wanted to kill and roast a goat for them, on the campus.'

It was round about this time that *he* asked me for a loan. I think that was behind the idea of bringing those pretty, dressed-up children along with him when he visited; he wanted firmly to set the background of his obligations and responsibilities before touching me for money. It was rather a substantial sum, for someone of my resources. But he couldn't carry on his job without a new car, and he'd just got the opportunity to acquire a really good second-hand buy. I gave him the money in spite of – because of, perhaps – new rumours that were going around then that, in a police raid on the house of the family with whom he had been living, every adult except himself who was present on that night had been arrested on the charge of attending a meeting of a banned political organization. His friends were acquitted on the charge simply through the defence lawyer's skill at showing the *agent provocateur*, on whose evidence the charge was based, to be an unreliable witness – that is to say, a liar. But the friends were promptly served with personal banning orders, anyway, which meant among other things that their movements were restricted and they were not allowed to attend gatherings.

He was the only one who remained, significantly, it seemed impossible to ignore, free. And yet his friends let him stay on in the house, it was a mystery to us whites – and some blacks, too. But then so much becomes a mystery where trust becomes a commodity on sale to the police. Whatever my little show of defiance over the loan, during the last year or two we have reached the stage where if a man is black, literate, has 'political' friends and white friends, *and* a passport, he must be considered a police spy. I was sick with myself – that was why I gave him the money – but I believed it, too. There's only one way for a man like that to prove himself, so far as we're concerned: he must be in prison.

Well, *he* was at large. A little subdued over the fate of his friends, about which he talked guilelessly as he had about the appropriation of Elias's air ticket, harassed as usual about money, poor devil, but generally cheerful. Yet our friendship, that really had begun to become one since Elias's death, waned rapidly. It was the money that did it. Of course, he was afraid I'd ask him to begin paying back and so he stopped coming to my 'place', he stopped the visits